Threads of Light

Stories from the World of The Second Coming of Grace

by Naomi Vondell

Threads of Light

Cover design and interior design by Naomi Vondell.

www.naomivondell.com

Some journeys begin not with a map,
but with a fracture.
These are the stories of finding the way through.

Everything Unsaid

The applause was a blur, just a roar in Liam's ears as he stepped off the stage with his diploma gripped in one slightly sweaty hand. His black gown clung to the back of his knees in the sticky June heat, and the mortarboard itched beneath the crown of his curls. He smiled anyway—smiled wide and bright and careful—because that's what you did when you were the golden boy. Valedictorian. Debate captain. Accepted to U of T with a scholarship. A boy any Oakville parent could be proud of.

He scanned the crowd. His father stood tall in the second row, clapping with the controlled dignity of a man used to being watched.

His mother dabbed under her eyes with a tissue, her gold necklace glinting in the overhead lights. To their left, two of his uncles beamed, and his little sister Clara snapped a photo on her phone.

And just behind them, leaning casually against the back wall, was Julian.

Julian wore a slightly wrinkled white button-down and the crooked grin Liam knew too well—the one that said, *I'm proud of you, and also, I'd like to drag you into a dark corner and kiss you breathless.* His hands were in his pockets. His brown eyes caught Liam's, held them, and something in Liam's chest fluttered.

The ceremony wrapped up not long after. Principal Sharma gave a few more words, the class tossed their caps, and the gymnasium erupted in chaos. Everyone was hugging. Crying. Laughing. Camera flashes bounced off the ceiling like strobe lights at a high school dance.

Liam posed for pictures, hugged his mom, shook hands with his dad. He thanked his aunt for the card and cash, accepted a bouquet from Clara, and smiled until his cheeks hurt.

And still—he was watching Julian.

At last, when the grownups turned to talk among themselves, Liam slipped away through the crowd. He found Julian waiting by the gym's side door, half in shadow. It smelled like summer out there—cut grass and pavement and the faint, sweet burn of barbecue from a nearby backyard.

"You made it," Liam said, breath catching.

"I said I would." Julian smiled and bumped their shoulders together. "You looked like someone's future Prime Minister up there."

Liam rolled his eyes. "Don't jinx it."

Julian reached for his hand but stopped short, glancing over Liam's shoulder. "Do we have a minute?"

"They're busy arguing about where to go for dinner," Liam said. "We've got at least five."

Julian didn't hesitate this time. He stepped in and wrapped both arms around Liam's waist. It wasn't rushed or desperate—just warm, grounding, real.

"You did it," Julian said softly. "You made it through."

Liam didn't mean for it to happen, but his throat tightened. "So did you."

And then Julian kissed him.

It was gentle, familiar—just a soft press of lips that tasted faintly of mint gum and something sweeter, like promise. Liam closed his eyes. The warmth of Julian's hands. The hush of the evening. The unspoken knowing between them.

Then—

A sound. The scrape of shoes on concrete.

A low voice, sharp with disbelief: "What the hell do you think you're doing?"

Liam's body went cold. His father stood just a few feet away, arms stiff at his sides, jaw clenched so tightly his neck cords stood out like wire.

Julian stepped back fast, his hands falling to his sides. "Mr. Russell—"

"Don't," Liam's father snapped. His eyes didn't move from Liam. "Is this a joke?"

Liam opened his mouth, but nothing came out.

"Is this what you've been doing all year?" his father went on, voice low and shaking. "Sneaking around behind our backs? Kissing boys behind the gym?"

"Dad," Liam said finally, throat dry. "Please don't—"

"Don't what?" his father barked. "Don't be upset that my son's been lying to me for God knows how long?"

Julian was already backing away, murmuring, "I'm sorry—I didn't mean—"

"Go," Liam whispered, his heart cracking. "Just go."

Julian hesitated. He looked at Liam like he wanted to say more, but then turned and disappeared around the side of the school.

Liam's mother appeared a moment later, flustered, holding her purse in a white-knuckled grip. "What's going on?" she asked, but when she saw Liam's face—really *saw* it—something shifted in hers. Her eyes flicked from him to his father and back again.

"We're leaving," his father said. "Now."

No one argued.

The car ride home was dead silent.

Liam sat in the backseat, still in his gown, the edges of the diploma folder digging into his palm. His mother stared straight ahead, eyes glassy. His father's knuckles were tight on the wheel, the only sound the occasional swipe of the wipers and the rhythmic blink of the turn signal.

When they pulled into the driveway, his father cut the engine and turned in his seat.

"How long?"

Liam stared at the back of the headrest. "I don't know. A while."

"You lied to us."

"No. I just didn't tell you."

"That's the same damn thing."

His mother finally spoke, voice small: "Liam…how could you not trust us?"

"I *wanted* to," he said, his voice cracking. "But you talk about people like me like we're broken. Like we're disgusting."

"You are not disgusting," his mother said quickly, but the words felt brittle—more reflex than conviction.

His father didn't answer. He just shook his head, once, slow and final.

"This isn't who you are," he said. "It's a phase. You've been confused."

Liam's chest tightened. "No, Dad. This is me."

"I won't have this under my roof."

His mother flinched. "David—"

"No, Lily!" he snapped. "Not in this house. I won't have our neighbours talking. I won't have our family embarrassed."

Liam felt something shatter inside him. Not like glass—more like the slow, inevitable collapse of a wall that had been barely holding itself up.

He opened the door and got out without another word.

The stars were out, but Liam couldn't see them. He sat on the edge of his bed, still in his dress shirt and slacks, gown tossed in a crumpled heap on the floor. The silence in the house was different now—dense, brittle, like something you could cut yourself on.

His phone buzzed.

Julian.

I'm sorry.

I thought we were alone. I never would've—

You looked so happy.

Liam stared at the screen for a long time, thumb hovering over the keyboard. He typed *It's not your fault*...then deleted it. He tried *I wish you hadn't*...then deleted that too.

In the end, he just set the phone down, screen still glowing, and turned it face down.

He couldn't tell if he felt numb or raw. Both, maybe.

The walls of his room felt like they were pressing in. The shelves with his soccer trophies. The honour roll certificates. The cross-stitched verse his mother had hung beside the door—*As for me and my house, we will serve the Lord.*

He stood and crossed to the window, pushing it open. Cool air rushed in, carrying the scent of lilacs and freshly watered lawns. Somewhere in the distance, someone was setting off fireworks—late, for graduation. A soft crackle of colour blooming invisibly behind the trees.

Liam wrapped his arms around himself and leaned on the sill. He wanted to cry, but the tears weren't coming. Only the ache, heavy and dull behind his ribs.

He tried to picture the future. University. A dorm room. A boy who could kiss him in broad daylight without fear.

It felt impossibly far away.

He sat back on the bed and reached for his journal. The leather cover was worn at the edges, the pages thick with folded thoughts and clumsy truths.

Tonight, he wrote:

I want to believe there's a version of me that gets to be whole. A version that doesn't flinch. Doesn't apologize. Doesn't lose everything every time he tells the truth.

I don't know how to get there yet.

But maybe tonight was the first step.

A soft knock at the door.

Liam didn't answer.

The door creaked open anyway, just a sliver, and Clara slipped in—barefoot, still in her pajama shorts and a Camp Wanakita T-shirt. She couldn't have been more than twelve, but she carried herself with that quiet, observant gravity that sometimes startled him.

Behind her padded a familiar shape—Charlie, their old mutt, part lab and part mystery, with greying fur and soulful eyes. His nails clicked on the floor as he ambled straight over and laid his head on Liam's knee with a huff.

Liam blinked hard.

"I heard fireworks," Clara said quietly. "I thought maybe you'd want company."

Liam couldn't speak. He reached down and buried his fingers in Charlie's scruff, letting the warmth of the dog's fur ground him. Clara climbed up onto the bed beside him without asking, curling her legs underneath her.

After a long pause, she asked, "Are you okay?"

"No," Liam said. Then, softer: "Not really."

Clara nodded, like that made sense.

"I think Mom is scared," she said. "But I'm not."

He looked at her.

"I don't care if you like boys," she added, like it was obvious. "You're still my brother."

That undid him. The tightness in his throat snapped, and the tears came, slow and silent, soaking into Charlie's fur. Clara leaned into him, small shoulder against his, and neither of them said anything more.

For the first time all night, Liam felt like maybe he wasn't completely broken. Maybe part of him was still intact—just cracked open.

The next morning, the house was silent in that strained, heavy way it gets when no one wants to be the first to speak. Liam came down to find the kitchen already empty, coffee mugs rinsed and left upside-down on the drying rack, chairs pushed in just a little too neatly.

Charlie's tail thumped once when he saw Liam, then stilled again as he laid his chin back on his paws.

Lily passed him in the hallway later, arms full of folded laundry. She didn't meet his eyes, but she paused long enough to murmur, "You need anything washed, just leave it by the machine."

It was meant to sound normal. It didn't.

David didn't speak to him at all.

The air inside the house felt colder now, like the thermostat had been turned down in more ways than one.

Clara didn't say anything either—but later that afternoon, Liam found a granola bar tucked into the side pocket of his backpack, along with a folded sticky note in purple marker:

You'll do great.

I'll miss you. 💜

P.S. Don't forget to call Charlie.

He sat on the edge of his bed for a long time with the note in his hands, running his thumb over the ink.

That evening, as the sun lowered behind the trees and the sky turned the colour of orange sherbet, he began to pack.

Not just for a night. Not just to cool things off.

For good.

Liam's bag wasn't heavy. A duffel and a backpack—that was all he took. Clothes, his journal, a few books, his laptop, and the framed photo of him and Clara in matching Harry Potter costumes from Hallowe'en two years ago. He left the trophies. The certificates. The cross-stitched verse.

He paused at the front door, hand on the knob. The house was dim behind him, still and echoing. From the living room came the low murmur of the evening news, David's voice occasionally rising in commentary. The sound had never made Liam feel more like a ghost.

Charlie padded into the hallway and looked up at him with soft, cloudy eyes. Liam knelt to wrap his arms around the dog's neck, pressing his cheek into the fur.

"Be good," he whispered. "You're the best part of this place."

He stood, and there was Clara at the top of the stairs, hugging the banister, her face half-hidden by the railing.

"I'll write you," he said. "Text me any time."

She nodded. "I will."

Neither of them said goodbye.

He opened the door and stepped into the cool evening. The last of the summer sun caught the edges of the clouds, turning them pink and gold. The cab he'd booked was waiting at the curb. He gave the driver a nod, then looked back one final time.

Lily stood just inside the storm door, arms wrapped around herself. She didn't come out. Didn't wave. But she watched.

It wasn't enough. But it was something.

The door clicked shut behind her.

Liam slid into the back seat of the cab, gave the driver the address of the sublet he'd found downtown, and leaned his head against the window.

He didn't know what his future would look like—not yet.

But the road was his now.

And he was finally, undeniably, on it.

The cast list had gone up sometime before dawn. Grace knew this because she'd barely slept, and by the time she reached the student lounge just past seven, three other first-years were already huddled in front of the corkboard, whispering excitedly and snapping blurry photos with their phones. It was a tradition at the National Theatre School—no online announcements, no email pings. Just a paper list, printed in 12-point Times New Roman, taped under the heading *Fall Mainstage: The Taming of the Shrew*.

Her name was there, third line down: **Kate – Grace Morgenstern.**

She froze. For a heartbeat, the letters seemed foreign, like she was looking at someone else's good fortune. But then her pulse quickened, and she pressed her fingertips against the paper as if needing to feel the ink.

Kate. She had done it.

It wasn't just any part. It was *the* part. Grace had dreamed of playing Kate since she was thirteen and saw a Stratford Festival broadcast on CBC. Kate had been fire and fury and wit and heartbreak, a girl who refused to be tamed until she decided, on her own terms, what love might mean. A girl who didn't shrink.

Grace had wanted to be that kind of girl.

She let out a soft, incredulous laugh. "Holy shit," she whispered.

"Congrats," said a voice behind her. She turned to find Philippe, a second-year tech student, sipping a Tim Hortons coffee and smirking. "Guess you'll be yelling at all of us from the stage now."

Grace grinned. "You wish."

"Check who got Bianca," he added, nodding toward the list.

Her eyes scanned the page again, lower this time.

Bianca – Sigrid Larsson.

Of course.

Sigrid, with her honey-blonde hair and cloudlike voice. Sigrid, whose Instagram grid looked like a curated lifestyle blog. Grace had once overheard a guest director call her "effortless." That word haunted her.

Kate was the better role, Grace told herself. The meatier one. The challenge. But as she stared at their names—*Kate: Grace Morgenstern. Bianca: Sigrid Larsson*—a tiny crack opened in her satisfaction.

Not fear. Not envy. Something quieter. Something that felt like doubt.

"This is going to be fun," Philippe said, already heading toward the cafeteria.

Grace stayed where she was a moment longer, the buzz of morning voices blurring around her.

She had won. But it didn't feel like triumph.

Rehearsals started with table work—a week of read-throughs, text analysis, and awkward icebreakers in Studio B. Grace arrived early every day, pencil case zipped with highlighters and sticky flags, script already dog-eared from obsessive re-reading. She wanted to be ready.

Prepared. Professional.

Sigrid drifted in ten minutes late on the first day, a cup of herbal tea in hand, her script pristine. She greeted everyone with warm cheek kisses like they were already old friends. Grace smiled back, stiffly.

Chase Dunbar was on time, at least. He wore a faded denim jacket and joggers, like he'd thrown on whatever was closest, but his energy filled the space. He wasn't loud—just... present. Like he assumed the room would shape itself around him.

They began with scene work: Kate and Bianca sparring. Grace threw herself into it. She layered Kate's lines with sharpness and bite, a shield made of syllables. Sigrid responded with a dulcet, trembling vulnerability that made the instructors swoon. Grace saw it. Saw how they leaned forward. Took notes.

By Wednesday, they were blocked into Act II. Grace and Chase were up.

He gave her a crooked grin. "Ready to tame me?"

She smirked. "Good luck with that."

But the moment the scene began, something shifted. The banter clicked. His energy met hers and didn't flinch. He pushed back, teased, provoked. It was like being dropped into a current—she had to swim or drown. And she swam. Her voice rang through the studio with something raw and alive, and when the scene ended, there was a beat of silence before the instructors clapped.

After rehearsal, he nudged her shoulder with his. "That was fun."

She tried not to smile too much. "Yeah. It was."

They walked out together into the chilly October air. Grace could see her breath fogging slightly in front of her. She hoped he couldn't see how fast she was breathing.

Grace hadn't expected the chemistry to last. She thought maybe it had been a fluke—one good run on one good day. But each time they ran scenes, it was there again: that thrum beneath the dialogue, the current running between them.

The rest of the cast began to notice. During breaks, people nudged each other and whispered when Grace and Chase took the floor. The instructors looked pleased. Even Sigrid, usually unbothered, had gone unusually quiet after one particularly electric run of Act IV.

"'Come, come, you wasp; i' faith, you are too angry.'"

Chase delivered the line with an amused glint in his eye, leaning just close enough that Grace felt it in her throat.

"'If I be waspish, best beware my sting.'"

She shot the line back like an arrow. The room laughed. Not at her—but with her. The moment rang with tension and mischief and something almost too bright to hold.

After rehearsal, Chase tossed his script into his backpack and said, "You hungry?"

She blinked. "Now?"

"There's that bánh mì place on Saint-Laurent. Come on, you've earned a sandwich."

It became a thing. Lunches after rehearsal. Coffee before warm-ups. The occasional text at night—quotes from the play, mostly, like an inside joke.

"'My tongue will tell the anger of my heart,'" he wrote one night.

Grace replied, "'Or else my heart concealing it will break.'"

She read that one three times before falling asleep.

For a while, it felt like something was unfolding. Not loudly. Not dramatically. But in small, deliberate gestures. A shared laugh. A lingering glance. An almost-touch backstage.

It felt like the beginning of something.

By November, the leaves in the courtyard had turned to papery husks, crunching under boots on the walk to morning call. Grace felt sharper in rehearsals, surer. She knew the shape of Kate's anger, the weight of her silence. But offstage, things had started to blur.

Sigrid and Chase had always gotten along. That wasn't new. What was new was how often they were laughing together now. How she'd catch Sigrid resting a hand on his arm during break. How they'd disappear for long stretches between scenes and come back flushed with laughter.

Grace told herself it was fine. That she and Chase had something else—something subtle. That the way he looked at her onstage meant something.

"'Am I not wise?'" he asked during a run-through, tilting his head at her, his grin crooked.

"'Yes, keep you warm,'" she snapped back, Kate's scorn slicing through her smile.

The room laughed again, but this time the air felt different. Like a current had shifted.

That Friday, after rehearsal, Grace lingered near the coat rack. Chase was talking with Sigrid across the room, their heads bent close. She waited. Fiddled with the cuff of her sweater. When she finally approached, Sigrid turned first.

"Oh hey! We're just heading to grab dinner," she said. "You coming?"

Chase looked up and nodded, friendly but distracted. Grace hesitated. Something in her chest tightened.

"No, I've got a scene to prep," she lied. "You two go ahead."

She walked home in the dark, the wind lifting her scarf and stinging her cheeks. Her phone buzzed once in her pocket—probably her mom. She didn't look.

The next morning, she arrived to find a photo on the class group chat: Chase and Sigrid at a tiny Italian café, arms draped over each other, both of them glowing. Someone had captioned it *Shrewmance?* with a string of heart emojis.

Grace stared at it for a long time before muting the chat.

Opening night. The house was full, the lights hot, the stage boards worn and painted black. Grace stood in the wings, the script gripped in one damp hand, listening to the rise and fall of dialogue from the stage. Her cue was soon.

She turned down the corridor behind the set, needing a moment to breathe. The backstage hall was dim, the sound of the performance muffled behind curtains and plywood. She rounded the corner—

And stopped cold.

Chase and Sigrid were locked in a kiss. Not hurried or nervous or accidental. Slow. Certain.

Sigrid's hands were in his hair. Chase pulled her closer with ease. Intimacy.

Grace stepped back before they saw her, retreating silently into the shadows. Her heart felt too big for her chest. Her stomach lurched.

"Places!" called the stage manager from somewhere nearby.

Grace walked calmly to her mark. Her hands no longer shook. They were steady. Cold.

The final scene began.

Chase—Petruchio—was there beside her, performing as if nothing had shifted. But for Grace, everything had.

Kate's monologue arrived. She stood centre stage, lit by a single spotlight, and began to speak.

"Fie, fie! unknit that threatening unkind brow, and dart not scornful glances from those eyes…"

Her voice was calm, clear. The pain beneath it ran like an undercurrent. She did not play submission. She played devastation with poise.

"I am ashamed that women are so simple…"

Her eyes didn't flick to Chase. They didn't need to.

"…to offer war where they should kneel for peace."

Grace stood tall. She did not kneel. Her Kate would never kneel.

"…place your hands below your husband's foot…"

Instead, she raised her hand, palm open, a symbol of giving what she chose, not what was taken.

"…in token of which duty, if he please, my hand is ready, may it do him ease."

Silence.

Then the audience burst into applause.

Backstage, the cast erupted with joy, but Grace moved like smoke through them. She didn't stop until she reached the green room hallway.

She turned a corner—and there they were again.

Sigrid, flushed. Chase, glowing.

Arms around each other. Laughing. Talking about summer theatre tours—London, maybe. Or Edinburgh.

They didn't notice her.

Grace didn't speak. She didn't cry. She just kept walking, the ache sharp and quiet in her chest.

She had delivered the performance of her life.

But the ending had never really been hers.

Sunday, September 7, 1986

The apartment smelled faintly of dust and old paint. Evelyn turned the key again just to be sure, then closed the door behind her. One suitcase, a small duffel, and a cardboard box marked *BOOKS – PSYCH & THEORY* sat in the middle of the linoleum floor like squat, indifferent guests. The radiator made a dry ticking noise.

She set her handbag down and crossed to the single window. The view was of a parking lot rimmed by yellowing grass and a few scraggly shrubs. Beyond that, a stand of maples edged the property, their leaves just starting to catch fire—splashes of red and orange flickering through the green. A grey sky pressed low against the rooftops.

Not bad, she thought. *Not good, but not bad.*

She filled the kettle and plugged it in, unsure whether to unpack first or sit down. The kettle let out a shriek she hadn't expected. She jumped.

There was a landline already installed, beige with a long curling cord. She picked up the receiver and dialed her mother's number in Thunder Bay. The line crackled once before the familiar ring.

"Hi, Mom. I'm here. Just got in."

"Oh good," her mother said. "Is the apartment decent?"

"It's fine. Tiny. Clean. Smells a little like storage." Evelyn smiled faintly. "I'm only here for the job, remember."

"You're lucky, getting something straight out of school. Lots of your classmates are still applying."

"I know."

Pause. Her mother clicked her tongue. "Don't let them walk all over you. These places eat quiet girls alive."

Evelyn didn't respond right away. "I'll be fine."

"Call me next week, eh?"

"Will do. Bye, Mom."

She hung up and stood there for a moment, one hand still on the receiver.

On the kitchenette counter was the manila envelope the hospital had mailed her a few weeks ago—her "onboarding package." It contained a map of the grounds, a printed staff directory, and a typed schedule with her name slotted under "Psych. Intern, Inpatient Rotation – Unit 1-D." No job description. No welcome message. Just a sticky note that read, *Report to Nurse's Station, Mon 8:30 a.m. – Q.*

She flipped the top page over. *Start Date: September 8, 1986.*

Class of '86, Lakehead University. That felt like a lifetime ago—and it had only been four months.

She walked back to the window. She noticed again that the row of maples near the lot had already begun to turn, the red just starting to bleed through the green like a warning.

The next morning, Evelyn arrived ten minutes early and still felt late.

She stood outside the heavy double doors of Unit 1-D, clutching the strap of her bag. The corridor smelled faintly of institutional soap and something older, like dust that had settled into the walls a long time ago and never fully left. There was a metal doorbell to the right—no sign, just a small white button. She pressed it.

A moment later, she heard the rattle of keys, and the door creaked open. A nurse in pale green scrubs gave her a quick once-over, then turned without a word and walked back toward the nursing station.

Evelyn followed, trying not to look lost.

The unit was L-shaped and dim. Fluorescent lights hummed overhead with the occasional flicker. Off the main hall, patient rooms branched out like ribs from a spine. A couple of people in hospital gowns shuffled past, one muttering to himself in a low monotone. Another stared straight ahead like she was looking through a window to hell.

The nurse returned to her spot behind the counter and picked up a black pen, scribbling into a large three-ring binder. The wall behind her was lined with shelves stacked with more patient charts, each one labelled in black marker on masking tape. A beige rotary phone rang once. She answered, said "1-D," and then, "One moment," before calling across the room for a doctor.

Evelyn hovered.

"Hi," she said. "I'm Evelyn Turner. I'm starting today—on my inpatient rotation?"

The nurse glanced up again. "Oh. Right." She looked around vaguely, then shrugged. "You can just hang around today. See how things run."

"Okay," Evelyn said, unsure what that meant. "Should I sit in on rounds?"

"If you want." The nurse returned to her binder.

A clipboard rested at the edge of the counter, and Evelyn reached for it instinctively, then hesitated. Was that allowed? She placed it back. A man in scrubs walked by without acknowledging her. He might've been an orderly or a nurse—there were no name tags.

She spent the morning drifting between the nurses' station and the common area, trying not to look idle. She perched on a chair during rounds but wasn't introduced. One man—mid-forties, ponytail, wire-framed glasses, jeans and sandals under a tweed blazer—spoke in a low voice, tapping a file with the back of his pen. He didn't look like any of her professors, but there was an ease to him, like he belonged in every room. She assumed he was a psychiatrist.

She scribbled notes in her notebook, though no one asked her to. Every time a door opened, she tried not to flinch.

By lunch, she hadn't spoken to a single staff psychologist.

At 1:15, she found an empty office labelled *Consult Room B,* sat at the desk, and opened a patient file. The fluorescent lights buzzed overhead. The file had no case formulation, just a series of medication changes and brief nursing notes. She underlined a phrase—*increased pacing noted in hallway*—and wrote *? Anxiety or akathisia* in the margin, as if anyone would ever see it.

Around 2:30, she wandered back to the main desk. The same nurse was still there.

"Should I check in with Dr. Quinn at some point?" Evelyn asked.

The nurse looked up. "You already did."

"I—sorry?"

"He saw you in rounds. Didn't say anything?"

Evelyn blinked. "I didn't know that was him."

The nurse smirked faintly, then turned her attention back to her notes.

Evelyn stood for another beat, then returned to the hallway and resumed walking. She tried to look like someone with a plan.

Evelyn sat at the fold-out table in her kitchenette, notebook open, pen poised. She'd made tea, though it had gone cold beside her elbow. Her bag lay on the floor where she'd dropped it, still half-zipped.

She drew a line across the top of the page and wrote:

Day 1 – Unit 1-D

Observations (Staff Dynamics)

She paused, then added: *Minimal orientation provided. Directed to "observe." No schedule or caseload assigned. Unclear who direct supervisor is.*

She frowned. That wasn't entirely true—Dr. Quinn had apparently seen her. Sat through rounds with her in the same room. Never said a word. And somehow, that counted.

She tapped the pen once, twice, then wrote: *Spoke with nurse re: Dr. Quinn—did not recognize him in rounds. Not introduced. Possibly deliberate?*

That last part felt like a leap. She crossed it out. Then rewrote it in smaller print beside it.

She flipped back a few pages to a set of neat notes from her last practicum placement. Structured timelines, names, referrals, supervision logs. She remembered how nervous she'd been at first—but also how supported. This was different. Here, she wasn't even sure what *doing a good job* would look like.

She glanced at the envelope from Bayshore still sitting on the counter. The schedule page fluttered slightly in the draft from the window.

Maybe it was just Day One. Maybe everyone was busy. Maybe she was overthinking.

But something about the nurse's smirk stuck with her.

She wrote: *Try to make contact with Quinn directly tomorrow.*

Underneath, in the margin, almost as an afterthought: *Figure out what "hanging around" is supposed to mean.*

She closed the notebook and went to bed early. Morning would come quickly. And she'd need to look like someone who belonged there.

Wednesday, October 15, 1986

A slip of paper was handed to her by a ward clerk with a mild shrug. "Dr. Quinn wants to see you. Office 3-A, main floor." No time given. Just an expectation that she'd figure it out.

She found the office mid-morning—past a locked med room, two fire doors, and a row of vending machines humming faintly in the corridor. The door was already ajar.

Dr. Quinn sat at a cluttered desk surrounded by teetering stacks of files, a mug stained with something once resembling coffee, and a poster of Carl Jung on the wall behind him, its corners curling. He wore a loose linen shirt over faded jeans and leather sandals. His hair was in a greying ponytail, and he didn't look up as she knocked.

"You're Evelyn," he said, still flipping through a file. "Sit."

She sat.

Dr. Quinn cleared his throat. "Have a nice long weekend?"

"Yes."

There was a long silence.

Finally, he closed the folder with a slow, deliberate motion and leaned back in his chair.

"I've observed you a few times on the ward," he said.

Evelyn straightened slightly. "Yes. I've been trying to orient myself, review the case files, get a sense of—"

"You wander around 1-D like a wraith."

The sentence landed with a thud in her chest.

"I—I'm sorry?" she said.

Dr. Quinn gave her a small, bemused smile. "You hover. You linger. You don't really engage. The staff don't know what to do with you. Neither do the patients."

"I wasn't given a caseload," she said, her voice tight. "I assumed there would be a more formal process, some kind of supervision plan—"

"This isn't school," he said, shaking his head. "We're not here to babysit you. You're an MA-level clinician in a functioning psychiatric facility. You're expected to act accordingly."

She nodded automatically, though her face burned. She wanted to ask what *acting accordingly* meant when no one had defined the role. But he was already opening another file.

"I suggest you try shadowing Dr. Pollack on B unit for a few days," he said. "1-D might be a little... intense for you."

Evelyn swallowed. "I'd like a chance to learn. I know I come across as reserved—it's something I've been working on—but I'm competent. I just need a clearer sense of—"

"We're not questioning your intellect," he said, with a wave of his hand. "You're obviously bright. That's not the issue."

She waited, but he didn't elaborate. Just sat there, watching her like a subject under glass.

"I'll check in next week," he added, already looking past her.

She stood slowly, unsure if she'd just been disciplined or redirected or quietly pushed aside. Maybe all three.

As she reached the door, he added without looking up, "Try to look like you have a purpose."

Evelyn walked out into the hallway, the door clicking softly shut behind her. She didn't cry. Not yet. Not until later, when she was alone in *Consult Room B*, staring at a file she couldn't read, because her vision had gone blurry.

Thursday, December 11, 1986

The common room on Unit 1-D smelled, as usual, of urine masked with lemon-scented disinfectant. Evelyn had started keeping a tin of mentholated lip balm in her pocket, just to dab under her nose before she entered.

Tinsel had been taped along the top of the whiteboard, drooping in the middle like a shrug. A miniature artificial tree stood on the corner table, its plastic needles bent from too many seasons in storage. Someone had drawn a snowman on the staff sign-in sheet.

Evelyn sat at a table by the window, flipping through a patient's binder, when Sandra Kapur slid into the chair beside her with a paper cup of tea.

Sandra was a social worker in her forties, with short, practical hair and kind eyes that didn't miss much. She'd spoken to Evelyn once or twice in the staff lounge—cordial, nothing more.

Now, she looked at the chart Evelyn was holding, then back at her face.

"You look like someone who's been told not to exist," she said softly.

Evelyn blinked. "I—I'm just trying to figure out where I fit here."

Sandra sipped her tea. "That's the problem. You're not meant to."

Evelyn frowned. "I don't understand."

Sandra glanced around the room. A patient was snoring lightly on the couch. Another stood by the window, mumbling to himself. No one was close enough to hear.

"Off the record," Sandra said. "You're the third."

"The third?"

"The third young woman they've slotted into this role. Dr. Quinn doesn't like working with women fresh out of grad school. Says they're 'overly idealistic.'" She made air quotes with one hand. "The other two didn't last six months."

Evelyn stared at her.

"Look, I'm not saying it's a conspiracy," Sandra added. "But don't expect mentorship. Or fairness. Or even logic. Just... know it's not about you."

A nurse passed by, nodding at Sandra. She smiled back, all warmth. The moment sealed itself in silence.

Evelyn lowered her voice. "Why are you telling me this?"

Sandra hesitated. "Because you still look surprised."

"I thought I was imagining it," Evelyn said. "I thought—maybe I was too sensitive. Maybe I didn't know how things worked yet."

Sandra gave her a sad smile. "Oh, you don't. But you're learning."

She stood, tossed her cup in the trash, and walked away, blending into the rhythm of the ward.

Evelyn stayed at the table, the chart open in front of her, though she hadn't read a word in ten minutes.

Tuesday, January 20, 1987

The windows in the staff lounge had frosted over from the inside. Evelyn pressed her hand against one and drew it back quickly, fingers stung by the cold.

The summons came in the form of a hallway comment. Dr. Pollack passed her near the medication room and said, "I'll need a word after lunch. My office."

No explanation. No greeting. Evelyn nodded, heart already fluttering.

She tried to eat a sandwich in the cafeteria but ended up picking it apart until the crusts curled. At 1:00 p.m. sharp, she knocked on the door marked *Dr. Renée Pollack, Staff Psychiatrist.*

"Come in," said a clipped British voice from within.

The office was small, windowless, and bright with fluorescent glare. A desk, two chairs, a calendar stuck on December, and the faint scent of old coffee. Pollack sat behind the desk with a folder open in front of her.

Evelyn stepped inside.

"Close the door, please."

She obeyed.

Pollack didn't look up. "There's been a complaint."

Evelyn tensed. "From...?"

"A patient on your outpatient caseload. Miss M. She says you don't listen."

"I—maintained a neutral expression," Evelyn said carefully. "That's what we were trained to do."

Pollack glanced up then, her tone perfectly level. "Yes, well. Some patients prefer to feel listened to rather than assessed."

She flipped the page.

"Patients are complaining about you."

Evelyn took a breath. "One patient."

Pollack's eyes narrowed slightly. "Well, we can quibble about actual numbers."

Evelyn blinked. "That's not really a quibble. It's plural versus singular. Not a matter of interpretation."

Pollack set the folder down and folded her hands. "Miss M has been reassigned. I've also recommended you be removed from Unit 1-D. Temporarily."

"I'm being taken off the unit because of one complaint?"

"I'm looking at the broader pattern," she replied crisply. "You've been... hesitant. Reticent. You hover in doorways. You don't quite enter the room, professionally speaking."

"I wasn't given any direction."

Pollack tilted her head. "Direction is not always on offer, Miss Turner. One must adapt."

There was a silence. Pollack's gaze never wavered.

"Will this be documented?"

"Not formally," she said with a slight lift of the brows.

Which, of course, meant it would be remembered.

"You may go."

Evelyn stood. Her legs felt oddly far away. The door closed behind her with a soft click.

She walked the corridor slowly, past the bulletin board where someone had pinned a curling poster about hand hygiene. Her pulse roared in her ears. She didn't cry—not yet.

That would come later, in a locked stall, with her coat still on and her bag on her knees.

Tuesday, February 3, 1987

The meeting was scheduled for 2:00 p.m. Evelyn arrived at 1:55, sat in the hallway outside the Chief Psychologist's office, and tried not to bounce her knee.

The union rep showed up two minutes late, holding a file folder and a tray of coffees he didn't offer to share. She didn't remember his name—Mike something?—but she'd seen him at a staff meeting once. He nodded at her like she was a stranger on a bus.

Dr. Mendes opened the door.

"Evelyn. Please come in."

His office smelled of dry paper and lemon floor cleaner. Two chairs had been placed opposite his desk. One for Evelyn, one for the rep.

"This won't take long," Mendes said, gesturing for them to sit. "Mike is here as union witness. Standard protocol."

Mike nodded and took out a notepad, but didn't write anything.

Mendes folded his hands on the desk. "We've had a few concerns raised about your clinical presence. A pattern of withdrawal. Lack of initiative. You're quiet in team meetings. Staff are unsure of your role."

Evelyn inhaled slowly. "No one told me what my role was."

Mendes smiled faintly. "This is a verbal warning, Evelyn. It's not disciplinary in the formal sense. But we do need to document the conversation moving forward."

She looked at Mike. He gave her a neutral glance and a small shrug, as if to say *This is how it goes.*

"I wasn't given a caseload. I wasn't given supervision. I've been trying to find ways to contribute. I've asked questions."

"Yes," Mendes said. "But there's also a perception."

She let out a quiet breath. "Perception isn't always reality."

Mike finally spoke, his voice low and bureaucratic. "Look, no one's accusing you of misconduct. But if you were thinking of filing a grievance—"

Evelyn blinked. "I hadn't said that."

"Well, I wouldn't recommend it," he said, expanding his hands several inches apart in the air. "You'll end up with a dossier *this big.*"

Evelyn stared at him.

"Just trying to give you the lay of the land," he added, as if he were doing her a favour.

Mendes nodded. "We're not looking to make this bigger than it is."

Then, almost casually, he added, "You've heard the saying, haven't you? *Give a dog a bad name and hang him.*"

Evelyn blinked. "I—sorry?"

"Perception, Evelyn. Once it takes hold, it tends to become... self-fulfilling."

She felt something in her stomach twist. Like a rubber band pulled too tight.

"That's all," Mendes said. "Thank you for coming in."

Outside the office, she didn't go back to Unit 1-D right away. She walked out through the staff entrance, into the parking lot, where snow was banked against the fence and the wind cut sideways across her cheeks.

She didn't cry. Not there.

Monday, March 16, 1987

The outpatient clinic had its own rhythm. Mornings were busy—patients, calls, reports. But by noon, the tempo shifted. Coats vanished from hooks. Coffee cups disappeared. A hush settled like snow.

Evelyn returned from the washroom to find her wing empty.

No Sandra. No nurse. No Dr. Pollack. No one had said a word.

A clerk at reception shrugged. "They all went out. Probably the Bluebird."

That was the little restaurant just across the street. Casual, vinyl booths, good soup.

She hovered by the door, unsure. The invitation hadn't included her—because there hadn't been one.

Still, Sandra's voice echoed from earlier in the month: *"You're not meant to fit in."*

But she had to try. Had to look like someone who didn't slink away at the first sign of exclusion.

She zipped her coat and headed across the slushy road.

Inside, she spotted them: Dr. Quinn, Dr. Pollack, Sandra, the nurse, and a case manager whose name she could never remember. They sat crowded into a booth, menus propped like shields. A bottle of red wine already sat open on the table.

Evelyn took a breath, pushed the door open, and approached the table.

"Hi," she said lightly. "I saw you'd all ducked out and figured I'd join you. Is that wine for the table?"

Dr. Quinn looked up from his menu. "Miss Turner," he said with mock solemnity, one brow lifted.

Something in his tone was just a shade too theatrical.

Evelyn nodded politely. "Dr. Quinn."

The case manager snorted. Dr. Pollack smirked. Even Sandra chuckled softly.

"'Dr. Quinn,' she says," he murmured, shaking his head. "I haven't been called that at this table in... what, six years?"

"Careful," added Dr. Pollack, dryly. "You'll make him feel ancient."

"I quite like it," he replied, raising his glass. "So formal. Miss Turner."

More chuckles. The name passed around like a balloon at a birthday party. Evelyn smiled tightly and slid into the booth, pretending not to feel her face burn.

She tried to keep her voice light. "I was starting to think I'd missed the memo."

Dr. Quinn raised his glass. "Apparently the memo was intercepted."

The others chuckled again.

Evelyn looked down at her menu and ordered soup when the server came. No one refilled her glass. No one asked her much of anything.

She ate quickly, made polite comments about the weather, and left before dessert.

Wednesday, March 18, 1987

Evelyn caught Sandra near the file cabinets that afternoon, while the rest of the team was in a consult.

"Can I ask you something?" she said, trying to keep her tone even.

Sandra turned, arms folded.

"Is there... any perception of me in the clinic I should be aware of? Anything I've done that's rubbed people the wrong way?"

Sandra hesitated. Her expression flickered—something quick and nearly invisible, like regret or recognition. A brief reminder of the woman who had once leaned in over a shared tea and said, *You're the third.*

Then it was gone.

"Well—if I'm being honest—some people thought it was a bit inappropriate when you invited yourself to lunch the other day."

Evelyn blinked. "Inappropriate?"

"You just kind of walked in and said, 'I'll have some wine, please.'

It came across a little... entitled."

"That's not what I said."

Sandra raised her eyebrows. "Maybe not word for word, but that was the impression."

A long pause.

"I didn't think I needed an invitation," Evelyn said quietly.

Sandra offered a tight smile, then turned and walked away.

Evelyn stood still, the silence louder than the hum of the copier behind her.

Wednesday, March 18, 1987

The walkway from the bus stop to her apartment was slick with grey slush. Her boots left wet impressions on the linoleum as she stepped inside. The radiator hissed and clanked in protest, and the air smelled faintly of old toast.

She didn't turn on the light. Just dropped her bag on the floor and stood there, her back to the door.

It was only 5:30, but the sky was already dark.

She sat at the fold-out table, coat still on, and opened her notebook.

Her eyes landed on a line she hadn't dared reread in weeks:

Tuesday, February 3, 1987

Verbal warning issued. "Pattern of passivity." No documentation. No recourse. Union rep advised against grievance. Mendes quote: "Give a dog a bad name and hang him."

Was that supposed to be a warning? Or a confession?

She stared at the words, unmoving. Her hand hovered over the page. Then, slowly, she picked up her pen and started a new entry:

Wednesday, March 18, 1987

Sandra laughed with them. That was the hardest part.

Maybe they've already made up their minds. Maybe they had, from the beginning.

She wiped her eyes, then added:

Note to self: Do not cry in front of them.

She closed the notebook, too quickly, like it might burn her fingers.

After a moment, she reached for the phone on the wall and dialed the number she'd copied from the back of the orientation binder weeks ago. The Human Rights Commission.

A woman answered. Polite, efficient.

Evelyn explained—haltingly—how she'd been given no direction, how her supervisor had made a disparaging comment, how a colleague had told her in confidence that she wasn't the first.

"Was this colleague willing to file a statement?" the woman asked.

"No," Evelyn said. "She said it off the record. And now... she's staying silent."

"And you're not a visible minority?"

"No."

A pause. "Unfortunately, without corroboration, and without a protected class designation, I'm not sure there's much we can do."

Evelyn said thank you and hung up.

She sat there for a while, the receiver still in her hand.

Then she picked it up again and dialed home.

"Hi, Mom."

A pause. "Everything okay?"

"I just needed to talk."

Her mother sighed. "What happened now?"

"I was... shut out. Then betrayed. Kind of. They've decided I don't belong."

Another pause.

"Well," her mother said, "maybe you're just not cut out for that kind of place."

Evelyn swallowed. "Maybe."

"Nothing wrong with admitting something's not a good fit. You don't have to prove anything."

"Yeah."

"I have to go," her mother added. "Dinner's on the stove. Call me Sunday."

"Okay. Bye."

She hung up slowly, then curled into herself on the kitchen chair as the wind pushed against the window.

The world had gone very quiet.

But somewhere deep in her chest, something had started to crack open. Not a scream. Not yet.

More like a question: *If they've already hung you, what's left to lose?*

Friday, March 20, 1987

The issue of *Topical* had nothing.

Evelyn sat at the staff lounge table with a stale muffin and the government's in-house job bulletin folded in half beside her. A few new clerical postings, two senior policy analyst roles in Toronto, and a part-time audiologist in Kenora.

Nothing for psych.

She scribbled a note in her daybook: *Check again next week.*

The fluorescent light above her buzzed intermittently. Someone had pinned a red paper heart to the bulletin board, already curling at the corners. Beneath it, a memo about hand hygiene and a signup sheet for a staff potluck she had no intention of attending.

She finished her tea, tossed the cup, and stopped by the payphone in the hallway before heading home. Her mailbox key stuck for a moment before turning with a metallic thunk.

Inside: a brown envelope with a return address she didn't recognize. Toronto.

She took it upstairs, removed her boots, and slit it open with a butter knife.

The letterhead was unfamiliar—**Willow Ridge Counselling & Wellness Clinic**.

Dear Ms. Turner,

Thank you for your interest in our associate counselling position. We would be pleased to invite you for an interview at your earliest convenience. While the position is located in Toronto, we are willing to conduct initial interviews by phone to accommodate your location...

She sat down on the edge of the bed and read it again.

Willow Ridge. She remembered now—it was one of the private clinic postings she'd circled in the *Toronto Star* classifieds two weeks ago, almost on a whim. She'd sent in her CV, not expecting a reply.

But here it was.

It wasn't government. It wasn't hospital. It wasn't even permanent—likely contract, fee-for-service. She'd have to relocate, figure out housing, navigate a new city.

But the letter addressed her as a professional.

Not as a problem. Not as a silhouette in the hallway. Not as a wraith.

She reached for the phone and dialed the number at the bottom of the page.

A warm voice answered on the third ring.

Monday, March 30, 1987

The summons came on hospital letterhead, slid into her department mailbox:

Meeting: Dr. Richard Mendes – March 30, 2:00 p.m.

Purpose: Employment Review

She folded the paper once, then again, and placed it neatly into her bag.

She knew what it was.

The call with Willow Ridge had gone well. The follow-up even better. The position was still part-time, but they liked her tone, her thoughtfulness. They valued her insight. She'd be starting in May.

It was enough.

She wore her navy blazer to the meeting—not the thick shoulder-padded one she hated, but the softer one, with the inner pocket where she'd tucked a folded copy of her new offer letter.

Dr. Mendes looked up as she entered. He smiled, warm and bland, as if they were old friends meeting for coffee.

"Evelyn. Thanks for coming. Please, sit."

The union rep wasn't present this time. She noted that. He wanted this to feel informal.

"How are you doing?" Mendes asked.

"I'm all right."

"Well," he said, leaning back, "we've reviewed your time with us over the past months, and there's been considerable discussion among the team. I won't draw it out. We've come to the conclusion that perhaps this placement isn't the best fit for your skill set at this time."

Evelyn reached into her bag, pulled out a single sheet of paper, and placed it on the desk between them.

"I've accepted another position," she said.

Mendes blinked.

It was quick—half a second, maybe less—but she saw it. The disruption. The moment when he realized she'd taken the narrative out of his hands.

"I'll be leaving the position effective April 24," she added. "My last official day will be the 23rd. I'll ensure everything's wrapped up."

Mendes picked up the letter and scanned it. "Private practice?"

"Community-based counselling clinic in Toronto."

"I see."

A pause. Then: "Well. I suppose that resolves things."

She gave a small nod.

"I appreciate you letting us know," he said, tone already sliding back into neutral. "Best of luck with your next chapter."

"Thank you."

He extended a hand. She shook it.

Then she walked out of the office with her back straight, her bag light on her shoulder.

In the hallway, she passed a staff bulletin board advertising the upcoming Easter bake sale. A cartoon rabbit held a basket of plastic eggs, its eyes too wide.

Spring was coming. Sort of.

A feather floated past the window, pale and slow. Evelyn watched it catch on a gust, hover, then disappear from view. The world had gone quiet again.

Evelyn, too, was drifting, but she was about to land.

And she was almost free.

Friday, April 24, 1987

She didn't say goodbye.

No cards. No cupcakes. No farewell lunch in the staff lounge with store-bought napkins and awkward small talk.

She'd already cleared her things the day before—her books, her mug, the little fern that hadn't quite survived the winter sun. What was left in her desk could stay.

She signed out at the end of the day, one last neat stroke of her pen on the clipboard at reception.

As she stepped outside, the air was soft and damp. Patches of dirty snow clung to the edges of the parking lot, and the grass was still a dull, matted brown. The wind no longer bit, but it carried the chill of meltwater and thawing ground.

Above her, a few skeletal branches showed the shy beginnings of life—one or two buds, small and tight and barely green, like they weren't quite ready to believe in spring.

She had almost forgotten what it felt like to hope for something and not be punished for it.

She turned once—just briefly—to glance back at the building.

The windows of Unit 1-D reflected the grey sky, opaque as ever.

She imagined her younger self inside, still walking those corridors with a clipboard and a neutral expression, trying to be whatever they wanted her to be.

You wander around 1-D like a wraith.

She exhaled slowly, and her breath left no cloud in the air. The frost had lifted.

"Let the wraith haunt someone else," she murmured.

And then she turned, stepped onto the bus, and didn't look back.

The Hardening

New York City, 1996

The elevator doors slid open with a hiss Krystle Bennett had already come to associate with possibility. She stepped onto the thirtieth floor of the MacLaren Talent Group, heels clicking like punctuation across the marble. Her reflection followed her in the glass walls—slim black trousers, cream silk blouse, a thrifted YSL blazer in navy that hugged her shoulders like it knew her ambition personally.

She looked the part. That was half the game, wasn't it?

The receptionist barely glanced up from her landline—cord coiled like a snake around her fingers—as Krystle passed. She made her way to her cubicle, a tidy corner near the Xerox machine, her desk graced by a fresh cup of coffee from the corner cart guy who flirted shamelessly and gave her the good Colombian beans because, as he once told her, *"You walk like you already own this city, Miss Mississippi."*

She didn't. Not yet. But she was working on it.

The city outside was grey and golden at once—morning sun diffused by smog, casting long shadows between buildings. She turned slightly, just enough to glimpse them: the Twin Towers rising in the southern distance, stalwart as hymnbook verses. She'd seen them on postcards as a girl in Hattiesburg. Now they were part of her skyline, steady in a way nothing else was.

She powered on her IBM ThinkPad, cracked open her day planner, and pulled a thick script from her shoulder bag. *Requiem for a City.* Title scrawled in Devin's fast, slanted handwriting.

She smiled despite herself.

A creak of polished shoes announced Gerry MacLaren's arrival. He passed her without stopping—just a lift of his thousand-dollar chin and a murmured, "Morning, Krystle," like she were another part of the décor.

She'd take it. Every inch of proximity mattered. Gerry was a gatekeeper, a schmoozer, a shark in Brioni, and she was going to learn from him. Until she surpassed him.

She sipped her coffee, watching the Towers shimmer between blinds. In the quiet beat before the phones began to ring, Krystle felt it: the city pulsing with promise. She would rise. She would not be sweet. She would not be stopped.

Café Vesuvio smelled like roasted garlic, red wine, and ink. A half-dozen playwrights, poets, and actors filled its mismatched chairs and wobbly tables, speaking in jazz-like rhythms over espresso and Chianti. It was the kind of place that didn't bother with menus. If you belonged, you knew what to ask for.

Krystle sat across from Devin Ashe, legs crossed, ankle bouncing beneath the table. She wore a vintage velvet dress in burgundy, collarbone bare, curls pinned up like she didn't care how perfect they looked.

Devin watched her with that sideways grin he always pulled when she surprised him—which was often. "You know," he said, tearing a piece of focaccia, "you still don't eat the crust."

She raised an eyebrow. "And you still try to make personality diagnoses based on my bread choices."

He laughed, deep and low. It hit her somewhere she refused to name.

On the bench beside him, a weathered messenger bag leaned against a bottle of San Pellegrino. From it, Krystle could see the corner of his script—creased, dog-eared, loved.

"I gave the script to MacLaren this morning," she said, voice carefully neutral.

Devin's eyes lit. "You did?"

"He won't read it right away," she warned. "But I will. Again. And Lola Santiago's coming to that Black Arts Collective reading on Thursday. If she likes what she hears..."

"She will," he said, no hesitation.

Krystle took a sip of her wine, grounding herself. "It's not just about the writing, Dev. It's about who they think will sell tickets. You know that."

He waved a hand, dismissive. "That's why I have you."

The words landed wrong—too easy, too comfortable—but she let them pass.

Instead, she leaned in. "You're brilliant. And I'm not going to let them water you down. I just need you to stay true to the work."

Devin reached across the table, traced the edge of her wrist with a single finger. "You know what I love about you?"

She didn't answer. She wasn't sure she wanted to know.

"You believe in things like they're unshakable. Like they've got roots."

Krystle blinked. The wine made her skin warm. "You say that like it's a flaw."

"No," he said, eyes steady. "I say that like I'm trying to remember how it feels."

Outside, a siren wailed down Houston. Inside, the candle between them flickered. Krystle looked at Devin and thought about her mama's hands kneading dough before church. About the sticky summer nights back home, listening to late-night jazz on the porch. About how far she'd come.

And how far she had to fall.

Lola Santiago's office was tucked inside a Beaux-Arts building with gargoyle cornices and a discreet brass plaque: **Santiago Arts & Entertainment**. Krystle had taken the subway uptown, heels swapped for runners until she was two blocks away. Then she changed shoes in the Tiffany lobby and reapplied her lipstick in the mirrored elevator.

Now, seated across from the grande dame of downtown theatre, she kept her breath even, her posture impeccable.

Lola herself was elegance and edge: a streak of silver in her dark curls, black wrap dress, red-framed reading glasses perched on the bridge of her nose. Behind her, a wall of framed playbills and production photos: Audra McDonald, Philip Seymour Hoffman, August Wilson scribbled into the corners.

"You're young," Lola said, flipping through *Requiem for a City* with long, lacquered nails.

Krystle smiled tightly. "That's temporary."

A pause. Lola looked up. Smirked. "Good answer."

The script sat between them on the desk, thick with possibility. Krystle had paper-clipped her annotated notes, scene breakdown, and a one-page summary that ended with: *This play does not pander. It sings.*

"I saw Devin Ashe read in the Village last year," Lola mused. "Did a monologue about his grandfather's radio getting stolen during the blackout. Had half the room crying."

"He's electric," Krystle said. "And the play's ready. We're still refining some dialogue, but structurally it's strong. No gimmicks. Just truth."

Lola leaned back, crossing one elegant ankle over the other. "Theatres want bums in seats, Ms. Bennett. And truth's only marketable if it's packaged right."

Krystle didn't flinch. "Let me show you how right it can look."

She slid a manila folder across the desk. Inside: a mock-up of marketing materials, a list of potential casting leads—including two actors Lola had produced before—and a draft production budget based on a small black-box venue.

Lola's brows lifted. "Well. You came prepared."

"I came with vision," Krystle replied.

For a moment, the only sound was the rustling of paper. Outside, a siren passed. Inside, the Towers stood somewhere to the south, quiet giants in the sky. Krystle had glimpsed them on the ride up, distant and serene, and thought: *Let me be steady. Let me be seen.*

Lola closed the folder. "I'll come to the reading. Thursday?"

Krystle nodded. "7:30. Black Arts Collective, Avenue B."

"Then we'll see if this vision of yours has legs." She smiled. "But either way, I suspect you do."

The house was packed. Folding chairs had been added in the back and people leaned against walls, bodies humming with that particular charge—like everyone could sense they were about to witness something real.

Krystle stood near the makeshift lighting rig, arms crossed, trying not to chew her cuticle. Devin was backstage, pacing and humming to himself. She could hear the low cadence of his voice threading through warm-ups with the actors.

Lola Santiago arrived five minutes before curtain, wrapped in a pashmina and trailing a cloud of sandalwood. She met Krystle's eye with a nod before slipping into a seat beside an off-duty *Village Voice* critic Krystle had intentionally invited.

Krystle exhaled.

Lights down. A hush. The first line landed—sharp, clean, resonant. The opening scene swelled with tension: a mother searching for candles during the blackout, a teenage son listening to the city breathe in the dark. The audience was hooked.

And Devin—God, Devin.

He read the narrator's role himself, standing off to the side like a conductor of memory. His voice slid into the crevices of the story, alive with ache, humour, and defiance. He didn't just read—he conjured. Every so often, he glanced at Krystle in the wings, and for those fleeting seconds, she believed in all of it. The show. The future. Him.

By the time the final line rang out—*"Even in the dark, we remember the light"*—the audience erupted. Applause thundered through the small space. Lola was on her feet. The *Village Voice* critic scribbled something quick and circled it.

Devin took a bow, flushed and shining. The cast filed offstage. Krystle moved through the sea of hands and congratulations toward him.

"You did it," she said, breathless.

We did it, she wanted to say. But she didn't.

He wrapped an arm around her waist, pulled her into a fast kiss, lips warm and wine-slick. "They loved it."

"They did," she echoed, dazed.

From behind Devin's shoulder, Krystle saw Lola approach, eyes glittering. "That was extraordinary," Lola said. "Let's talk this week. I have a slot at the Public for fall."

Krystle's throat caught. "Yes. Yes, of course."

Devin was already mid-laugh, already moving on to the next person, the next glass of cabernet. Krystle stood still in the eye of the storm, her pulse like a jazz rhythm, syncopated and rising.

She didn't notice, just yet, how he didn't reach for her hand.

Didn't notice the woman who greeted him by name and lingered a little too close—*Marina,* her mind would recall later. Assistant director. Or co-director? That hadn't been discussed.

Not yet.

But the crack had started. The applause had covered it. And for one glittering, dangerous moment, Krystle let herself believe this was the beginning of everything.

The office was warmer than Krystle remembered. A radiator clanked beneath the windows, exhaling dry heat into the air. Lola Santiago sat behind her desk, silk scarf coiled at her throat like a signature.

Krystle was early. Devin was late.

"So," Lola said, pouring herself a splash of Perrier, "the board loves it. The artistic director's already envisioning press photos. But there are… conversations happening."

Krystle's spine straightened. "Conversations?"

"Funding partners," Lola said smoothly. "They're excited, but cautious. You know how it is. One of the backers—a big fish from Park Avenue—had some concerns about tone. About whether the piece might alienate some of our subscription audience."

Krystle didn't flinch. "You mean the white audience."

Lola gave a little smile, unbothered. "I mean the donors who keep the lights on."

She leaned forward, tapping a manicured finger on the manila folder between them. "They're asking for a few adjustments. A second director, to co-helm. Someone with experience navigating press, unions, opening night logistics."

"And who fits their image better," Krystle said, voice tight.

"Marina Firth," Lola replied. "She's smart. And she's already read the script."

Krystle's jaw twitched. "Devin hasn't agreed to that."

"He will," came Devin's voice from the doorway.

He entered casually, leather jacket slung over one shoulder, no apology on his face. He kissed Lola's cheek, sat beside Krystle, and didn't look at her.

"You knew?" she asked.

"I met with Marina yesterday," he said. "She had good ideas."

"You went behind my back."

"It's not like that," he said. "Lola needed movement, so I moved. This is how the business works, Krys."

Her mouth opened. Closed. "You said you wouldn't let them dilute the story."

"They're not. I'm just making it palatable."

Krystle felt it then—a shift, tectonic and silent. The room kept spinning, the radiator kept clanking, Lola kept sipping Perrier. But the shape of the world changed.

He'd already decided. Without her.

And he was fine with it.

"Thank you both for coming," Lola said, standing. "We'll send through the contract by end of week."

Krystle rose, slowly, deliberately. "If you think I'm going to roll over and let this happen—"

"No one's asking you to roll over," Lola said. "But maybe… adjust your posture."

It was said gently. Like advice.

Krystle nodded once. Then turned and walked out, heels echoing on the parquet floor.

She didn't look back.

Krystle walked south until the buildings thinned out and the river came into view, dusky and vast. The Staten Island Ferry lumbered past in the distance, orange paint faded, horn low and lonely. She kept walking. Past couples curled on benches, joggers in nylon, an old man feeding pigeons with surgical precision.

She reached the edge of Battery Park and sat on a granite ledge facing the harbour, elbows on her knees, blazer wrinkling at the sleeves. The Twin Towers rose behind her, reflected faintly in the glass of the kiosk selling hot pretzels. She didn't turn to look. She didn't need to. She could feel them—still and monumental—like they were keeping vigil for her.

She exhaled, slow. Counted it out: four in, hold for four, four out. Ground yourself. Don't cry in public.

Marina. She'd worn a cream blouse and black pants at the reading, like she was already part of the crew. Hair slicked back in a bun that said *I belong here.* She'd smiled too long when Devin introduced them—*This is Marina, she's interested in the production*—and Krystle had smiled too, gracious, strategic, while something ancient turned in her gut.

Good ideas, Devin had said.

He didn't used to talk like that. He used to call compromise a disease. He used to say Krystle's edits made him better. He used to touch her like she was home.

The wind picked up, carrying the scent of salt and asphalt. She pulled her coat tighter.

Somewhere back in Mississippi, a kitchen fan squeaked in rhythm with her mother's voice. *Baby girl,* she'd said once, while straightening Krystle's collar before church, *you're going to have to work twice as hard to get half as far, and then smile while you're doing it so they don't call you bitter.*

Krystle had been eight. She'd asked, *Why?*

Her mother had kissed her cheek. *Because they expect you to lose. But you don't have to hand it to them.*

Krystle clenched her jaw.

She had handed them something. Her instincts. Her trust. Her vision.

And now Devin would share credit with someone safer. Someone paler. Someone who didn't come up from the Delta with dollar-store shoes and a library card that was her best friend.

She didn't know if he was sleeping with Marina. Not yet. But the betrayal was already there. It lived in his silence. In his yes without her.

The sun dipped lower, setting fire to the river. Krystle finally turned. The Towers stood tall against the orange haze, like they'd been carved from resolve.

Protect your position before your passion, she thought.

It wasn't a motto. Not yet.

But it was beginning to sound like prophecy.

Krystle hadn't meant to go. She'd told herself she was just dropping off the actor's release forms with Devin—quicker than mailing. Cleaner. But part of her, the part still wearing hope like perfume, wanted to see him. To watch him look guilty. Or grateful. Or even ashamed.

Anything real.

She buzzed the loft once. No answer. Again. Nothing.

She was about to turn away when the door clicked open.

It was Marina.

Barefoot. Wearing one of Devin's band T-shirts. Eyes widening a little too late.

"Oh," she said, voice soft and unsure. "Krystle. Hi."

Krystle stared. Said nothing.

Marina stepped aside. "He's—he's here, he's just—"

But Krystle was already walking past her. The loft smelled like incense and cheap red wine. There were pages of *Requiem* on the coffee table, annotated in unfamiliar handwriting. A bra slung casually over the back of the couch. A Miles Davis record playing low in the background—one Krystle had given him for his birthday.

Devin came out of the bedroom, shirtless, pulling on a pair of jeans.

He froze.

"Krystle."

"You left your mail at the agency," she said, holding up the manila envelope. "Figured you'd want it."

He opened his mouth. Closed it. The silence throbbed.

She walked over to the coffee table, set the envelope down with surgical precision. The record popped faintly under Miles's trumpet.

"Looks like you two are settling in," she said.

"Krystle—"

"No. Don't." She turned to face him fully. "You could've said something. You could've had the decency."

Devin looked cornered, boyish, pathetic. "It wasn't planned. We were working late and—"

"And you just fell onto each other?"

He didn't answer.

Behind her, Marina slipped into the bedroom, the door clicking shut like punctuation.

Krystle stared at Devin. Not the man she'd loved, but the boy he still was. Charming. Insecure. Opportunistic. She saw it now. All of it.

"You're going to make it," she said quietly. "The play's good. And you've got people willing to make it palatable."

He winced.

"But I won't be part of it."

"Krystle—come on. Don't do this. Don't throw it all away because of—"

"No," she said, steel in her spine. "You threw it away."

She left before he could answer. Out the door, down the steps, onto the street where the air was sharp with February's breath. She didn't cry. Not this time.

Instead, she walked. Past galleries and bodegas. Past a couple kissing against a lamp post and a woman hailing a cab in Louboutin heels. Past it all.

The Towers shimmered in the distance, ghost-pale against the night sky. She didn't stop walking.

The office smelled like toner and ego.

Krystle sat at her desk, typing with quiet precision, her gold pen balanced between her knuckles. The script for *Requiem for a City* lay in a drawer. She hadn't opened it since the night she walked out of Devin's apartment. She wasn't angry anymore.

She was done.

Gerry MacLaren appeared in her periphery, barking something into a cellphone and laughing like he owned the zip code. He glanced her way.

"You good with that sitcom kid?" he asked, still scrolling.

"Locked in," she replied. "Network deal's clean. No riders, no parental drama."

He gave her a nod. "You're sharp, Bennett. You're going to last."

She didn't smile. "I don't plan to just last."

When he walked off, she opened her planner, scratched out the next hour's slot, and replaced it with a note: **Research legal pathways to become independent.** Beneath that: **Lunch with Kwan – potential producer contact.**

She pulled out a headshot from a new client—a young Black woman from Atlanta with fire in her eyes and a monologue about gentrification that had made Krystle sit up straighter the first time she heard it. Not polished. Not palatable. But brilliant.

Krystle opened a new file. Started drafting a plan.

She no longer believed in happy endings. She believed in leverage.

At lunch, she walked down to Battery Park again—this time in heels that clicked like punctuation and sunglasses that hid everything. She sat on the same granite ledge and ate her sandwich in silence, watching a tugboat drift toward Staten Island.

The Towers stood in the distance, unmoved by weather or whim. They were just there. Like truths no one could scrub out.

Krystle pressed a hand to her blazer pocket. Inside was the last letter Devin had ever written her, folded in quarters and creased from rereading.

She took it out. Smoothed it once. Then, without ceremony, tore it into strips and fed them into the wind. They scattered like smoke, like old scripts no one would ever stage again.

She stood.

She would not be softened. She would not be sidelined. And she would never again let anyone call her bitter for refusing to shrink.

The Towers loomed steady behind her as she walked back toward the future—heels high, jaw set, no-nonsense and fireproof.

Toronto, 2005

The office was quieter than she was used to—less hustle, more hush. From the window, Krystle could see the CN Tower rising above the skyline like a compass needle, steady in the grey.

It wasn't New York. But that was the point.

She flipped open the day's file: a new playwright out of Vancouver, edgy and unafraid. Her kind of risk.

On the shelf behind her, tucked between binders and glossy headshots, sat a single keepsake: a creased playbill from *Requiem for a City*. Faded ink. Still legible.

She hadn't spoken to Devin since the week of the opening. He went west. Did a stint in L.A. Wrote for television. Someone once told her he won an award. She hadn't Googled it.

She'd already left New York by then. After the towers fell, she couldn't breathe there anymore. The city that once stood like scripture had become rubble, smoke, and silence.

So she came north. Started over.

Rebuilt with steel of her own.

Her assistant poked in. "Krystle? You've got five minutes before the Tisch call."

Krystle nodded. "Thanks."

She took one last look out the window—at the tower, the sky, the strange stillness of safety—and turned back to work.

There were stories to protect. And this time, they would not slip through her hands.

Trois-Rivières, Quebec – Autumn 1943

The cathedral bell rang out over the rooftops of Trois-Rivières, cutting through the grey morning like a blade of sound. Celeste Dufour paused outside the épicerie, her gloved fingers tightening around the handles of her basket. The bell always struck at precisely eight o'clock, as if God himself needed reminding of the hour.

She didn't mind the sound. It was solid. Familiar. She could feel it in her ribs, like the thump of her own heartbeat. But some days—especially ones like this, when the air pressed low and the Saint

Lawrence smelled of smoke and metal—she wondered if the bell rang to wake the faithful... or to keep them in line.

Inside the shop, Madame Laurier was already gossiping with the butcher's wife. Celeste dipped her head in polite greeting, collected a sack of flour and a tin of milk, and placed her ration stamps on the counter with quiet precision. She had grown good at quiet. It was the only way to be heard in her house.

The war had taken more than food and fabric. It had taken her father last winter, in a place she couldn't pronounce, and her older brother Jacques in the spring—though his death hadn't been confirmed. Her mother lit candles for them both every Sunday, face pale in the golden light, lips moving in Latin. Celeste prayed too. But lately, her words felt like paper airplanes launched at a brick wall.

Outside again, she didn't go straight home. The path curved around the cathedral, its high stone spire scraping the overcast sky. She paused at the gate, letting her fingers brush the iron. Through the bars she could see schoolchildren playing in their uniforms, laughing, jostling. One girl had a red ribbon in her hair. It fluttered like a flag.

Celeste reached into her coat pocket and touched the pressed maple leaf tucked into her prayer book. Its deep crimson veins looked almost painted. She didn't know why she'd saved it, only that when she found it, she'd felt something—a hush, a stillness. Like someone had whispered her name in a language older than French.

She walked on, basket swinging gently at her side, as the cathedral bell struck once more—this time, not with command, but with invitation.

Later that day

The rain began in a hush, barely more than mist. By the time Celeste reached Rue Saint-Louis, it had thickened into a curtain. She darted beneath an awning, the wicker basket bumping against her hip, and found herself in front of a shop she didn't recognize.

Librairie d'Occasion – Livres rares et oubliés.

The sign above the door was hand-painted, the gold lettering cracked and fading. In the foggy window, a display of lopsided stacks leaned against glass smudged with time. The door was slightly ajar, as if expecting her.

She hesitated—then stepped inside.

It smelled of old paper, lavender, and something earthy, like damp stone. The light came from a single hanging bulb that swung ever so slightly, casting shadows across shelves too tall for her to see over. Books spilled from crates and nooks in no particular order. A porcelain cat watched her from atop a stack of encyclopedias.

"Bonjour?" she called softly.

No answer.

Drawn forward, Celeste ran her fingers along the spines of forgotten titles. Faded poetry collections. Wartime memoirs. A cookbook in Provençal dialect. Then, half-buried beneath a ledger and a hymnal, she saw it.

A small, clothbound book in deep indigo, the cover stamped with a symbol—part flower, part flame.

She pulled it free. The title, pressed in gold, was nearly rubbed away: *Les Voix de l'Invisible.*

Beneath it: *par Colette de Vannes.*

She opened it at random. The text was in flowing, elegant French—not printed, but handwritten, as though copied with care. Beside the words were delicate drawings of stars, herbs, and sigils she didn't recognize. A phrase caught her eye:

"Toute vérité est d'abord un murmure. Il faut apprendre à écouter entre les battements du cœur." (All truth begins as a whisper. One must learn to listen between the heartbeats.)

The sound of footsteps startled her. An old woman with a silver braid appeared from behind a curtain. Her eyes, pale and slightly clouded, blinked in recognition.

"Pour toi, celui-là," she said simply, gesturing to the book in Celeste's hands. "Il t'attendait."

Celeste fumbled in her coat pocket for coins. "Combien?"

The woman shook her head. "Un sou. Pour la forme."

Celeste passed over a single coin. The woman tucked it into a porcelain dish without looking.

As Celeste turned to leave, the woman added, almost as an afterthought, "Elle écrivait pour les vielles âmes. Tu comprendras bientôt."

Outside, the rain had lightened to a mist again. Celeste held the book to her chest, heart thudding—not with fear, but something else. A pulse of knowing. As though the air itself had shifted, and something long asleep inside her had stirred.

That evening

The smell of yeast and woodsmoke filled the house. Celeste slipped through the front door just as her mother let out a huff of breath and slammed a lump of dough onto the floured table.

Thud.

"You're late," Madame Dufour said, without looking up. Her sleeves were rolled to the elbow, hair pinned in a way that dared gravity to interfere. "Did the épicerie run out of flour again?"

"No, Maman." Celeste placed the groceries carefully on the counter. "Madame Laurier just talks a lot."

Thud.

Her mother lifted the dough like a prized adversary and slammed it again, harder. "She always has. Even as a girl, that one was more mouth than sense."

Thud.

Celeste pulled off her coat and slipped the indigo book into the folds of her prayer book before placing both in the sideboard drawer. She doubted her mother would notice—her gaze rarely drifted far from the stove or the crucifix over the kitchen door. But still, better hidden.

"You'll help with the soup," her mother said, attacking the dough anew. "Your Uncle Claude is coming tomorrow. We need to be ready."

"Of course." Celeste fetched carrots and began peeling. The rhythmic scrape of blade on skin layered over the percussion of kneading dough. *Scrape. Thud. Scrape. Thud.* The house sounded like an old marching song no one wanted to sing.

The book called to her from the drawer. She could feel it, like a gentle tap on the shoulder that never came.

Her mother paused to wipe flour from her brow. "And don't forget to bring in the laundry before supper. Unless you want the neighbours thinking we're pagans."

Celeste almost laughed. *If only you knew.*

Later, after the bread was shaped and rising beneath a damp towel, Celeste retreated to her bedroom under the sloped eaves. The wind tapped lightly at the windowpane. Somewhere outside, a dog barked once, then went quiet.

She opened the prayer book, lifting the hidden indigo volume free.

Page after page unfurled like a language she had always known but never spoken. The script was a mixture of reflection and instruction, sometimes poetic, sometimes riddling. It spoke of inner worlds and unseen guidance, of symbols that shimmered at the edges of waking life.

"Certains chemins ne se voient qu'avec les yeux fermés." (*Some paths can only be seen with eyes closed.*)

She paused, fingers pressed to the phrase. The candle beside her flickered once—no draft. She leaned closer.

A whisper seemed to move through the room.

Not a voice exactly. More like a suggestion. A breath against the fabric of her thoughts.

Celeste blinked and looked around. Everything was still.

She laughed quietly to herself, closed the book, and slid it under her pillow.

Below, in the kitchen, her mother was singing an old lullaby—off-key and with great feeling—while banging the soup pot with a wooden spoon.

The next evening

Uncle Claude arrived with the smell of pipe tobacco, wet wool, and something faintly medicinal. His hat was two decades out of fashion, and he wore it indoors as if daring anyone to mention it.

"Ma belle nièce!" he bellowed, arms wide. "Look at you—taller than a beanpole and twice as serious!"

Celeste offered a small smile as he pulled her into a bear hug that smelled like his overcoat had been baptized in gin.

He stepped back and wagged a finger. "You've got your mother's eyes, but your father's slouch. Stand tall, for God's sake. The world already wants to trample you."

Her mother emerged from the kitchen, apron immaculate despite the flour streak on her cheek. "Claude, don't lecture the child. Sit. Supper's ready."

Claude made a grand production of removing his coat, then collapsed into the high-backed chair at the head of the table, as though claiming a throne no one else had asked for.

The meal was humble—bread, potato soup, a little pork—but

Celeste's mother had folded in thyme and browned the onions just right. Claude slurped heartily, sighing after every bite as though no one had fed him since Easter.

Between spoonfuls, he launched into tales of misadventure at the paper mill, of a coworker who'd lost two fingers to a machine but gained a sweetheart. "The girl's a nurse, so she sees him as a project," he explained, raising his eyebrows. "You'd be amazed what love can do with a stump."

Celeste stifled a laugh in her napkin. Her mother glared.

But the air shifted when Claude set down his spoon and reached for his glass.

"I saw Jacques once," he said quietly. "Not long before he shipped out. He looked just like Jean did, before the war took the light out of him."

The table fell silent.

Celeste's mother folded her hands. "We've had no letter."

Claude nodded. "Doesn't mean he's gone. But the front… it's a graveyard with moving parts."

They sat with that a moment, the soup cooling in their bowls.

Then Claude raised his glass. "To the Dufour men—wherever they may be. And to you women, for keeping the hearth lit."

Celeste clinked her glass gently to his. Her mother hesitated, then did the same.

As the night wore on, Claude told stories with more laughter than logic. He recited a dirty limerick in bad Latin, insisted the cat was possessed, and offered to teach Celeste how to swear in six languages ("for self-defence," he claimed). But every so often, he'd glance toward the window, where the night pressed against the glass like a question no one wanted to answer.

When he finally left—hat askew, singing a soldier's march under his breath—Celeste stood at the window and watched his figure blur into the shadows.

He hadn't asked her about school. Or her dreams. Or the book under her pillow.

But something in the way he'd raised his glass had made her feel… seen. Like a person, not just a daughter left behind.

That night, the wind rose and rattled the shutters, but inside Celeste's room, all was still. She curled beneath her quilt, the indigo book tucked under her pillow like a secret. Sleep came slow and full of shadows.

Then, the dream.

She stood at the edge of the Saint Lawrence, though it was wider than she remembered—an inland sea, silver under a moonless sky. Mist clung to the water, rising in tendrils like smoke from a censer.

Across the river, a light flickered. Then another. A dozen tiny flames, hovering in the air like candles without hands.

She stepped forward. Her feet didn't touch the ground. The river wasn't water now—it was velvet, or sky, or memory.

Something moved beside her.

She turned, but saw only a figure in silhouette. Tall, robed, genderless. The face shimmered—there and not there, like a reflection glimpsed in passing.

The figure raised one arm and pointed to the sky.

Above them, stars rearranged themselves into a pattern she didn't recognize. Circles and lines, a kind of map. A sigil?

The figure spoke, though the voice didn't come from its mouth. It came from everywhere.

"You are not lost, child of breath."

Celeste felt the words in her chest, like a tuning fork had been struck inside her. She tried to speak, to ask what it meant—but her mouth wouldn't open.

Then the scene shifted.

She was back in the bookshop, but it was darker now, and the books whispered as she passed. The old woman with the silver braid stood behind the counter, her eyes milky white.

"Il faut apprendre à écouter entre les battements du cœur," she said. (*You must learn to listen between the heartbeats.*)

Celeste reached for the indigo book on the table—but it opened itself.

Pages turned in a rush. Symbols. Stars. A tower falling. A woman crowned with the moon. A path leading through a forest of eyes.

Then—a bell. Low and deep, vibrating through the dream like thunder under water.

She woke with a gasp.

Her room was dark, her hands clenched around the quilt. The

book still rested beneath her pillow, warm to the touch.

Downstairs, the wind knocked a shutter loose. But inside her, something new had taken root. Not fear.

A question.

And the quiet, undeniable feeling that someone—or something—had begun to answer.

It was cold enough that morning to turn breath into fog. Celeste walked quickly, scarf wrapped tight and thoughts still tangled in the dream. The river, the figure, the bell—it clung to her like smoke, impossible to brush away.

At the schoolyard gate, she spotted Lucie Tremblay, her oldest friend and most reliable source of both sense and nonsense.

Lucie was hunched beneath the statue of Saint Marguerite, trying to light a cigarette with a match she struck on the stone base. Her wool stockings had a run in them, and her hat was askew, as usual.

"You'll get caught," Celeste said, stepping up beside her.

Lucie exhaled triumphantly as the tip flared orange. "Then at least I'll die warm."

Celeste smiled in spite of herself.

They walked toward the side entrance, skirts snapping in the wind. Lucie passed the cigarette between them like communion. Celeste didn't inhale, but she liked the ritual of it—the camaraderie of doing something small and mildly forbidden.

"You look like you've seen a ghost," Lucie said, squinting at her. "Or had a dream about one."

Celeste hesitated.

Lucie raised an eyebrow. "I was joking."

"I did have a dream," Celeste said slowly. "A strange one."

Lucie grinned. "You always have strange dreams. Last year it was flying eels, remember?"

"This one was different. It felt… important."

Lucie leaned in, intrigued. "Go on, then. Did an angel give you your future husband's name? Please tell me he's tall."

Celeste shook her head, but her smile faltered. "It wasn't like that. There was a river. And a figure—someone not quite human. The stars moved. They made… a kind of pattern. And there was a bell."

Lucie blinked. "That's either very holy or very insane."

"I think it was a sign."

Lucie was quiet for a moment, then offered the cigarette again. "Well. If you start hearing voices, write them down. I could use the excitement."

Celeste didn't laugh this time.

Lucie sighed and slung an arm over her shoulder. "I'm teasing. Mostly. But you know how people are around here. If you start talking about stars and river spirits, you'll get more than side-eye. You'll get prayer circles."

"I'm not going to tell everyone. Just you."

Lucie gave her a gentle squeeze. "Then I'm honoured. Seriously."

They reached the school doors and stomped the snow from their boots. Before stepping inside, Lucie paused.

"Maybe the dream means you're meant for something different," she said. "More than this place. I don't know what, but... I've always thought you were a little bit magic, Dufour."

Celeste blinked. No one had ever said that to her before—not even in jest.

"Thanks," she whispered.

Lucie shrugged. "Don't let it go to your head. Unless it gets you out of math class."

The Saint-Martin Autumn Fair was mostly an excuse for people to gather and pretend the world wasn't at war. Children ran through the makeshift stalls with sticky fingers and flushed cheeks, parents bartered for knitted mittens and preserves, and accordion music battled the cold with stubborn cheer.

Celeste walked beside Lucie, who had traded her usual sarcasm for open delight. She pointed out a boy she claimed to be in love with ("but only until Tuesday"), then dragged Celeste toward a stand selling caramel apples.

They wandered past hand-stitched quilts, jars of cloudy honey, and a priest blessing harvest baskets with a bundle of wet cedar.

That's when Celeste saw the tent.

Small, striped, and tucked behind the main row of stalls, it looked older than everything else. A crooked sign above the flap read:

Lectures de Tarot – Destin et Vérité

Celeste slowed.

Lucie noticed. "Oh no. You're not actually thinking—"

"I just want to look."

"You'll end up married to a goat farmer in Lévis."

But Celeste was already walking toward the tent.

Inside, the air was warm with incense. A woman sat at a low table, her hair wrapped in a patterned scarf. She had dark, heavy-lidded eyes and long fingers that moved like dancers as she shuffled a deck of cards.

She looked up as Celeste entered.

"Entrez, ma petite. You're just in time."

Celeste hesitated. "How much?"

The woman smiled. "For you? Just the truth."

Lucie snorted behind her. "I'll wait outside. Try not to sell your soul."

Celeste sat.

The woman placed the cards between them and gestured. "Cut."

Celeste did.

Three cards were drawn and placed in a line.

The Tower. The High Priestess. The Star.

The woman said nothing for a long time. Her expression shifted subtly, like someone listening to music only she could hear.

"You've begun something," she said at last. "Though you do not know its name. A path has opened—one walked in silence, lit by stars."

Celeste stared at the cards.

"The Tower," the woman said, tapping the first. "Destruction. But necessary. What crumbles makes way."

"The High Priestess. You feel her already. The voice between heartbeats."

Celeste's breath caught.

"And The Star. Hope. Not safety—but clarity."

The woman looked up, her eyes suddenly sharp. "You won't stay here. Not forever. Your roots are deep, but they are not chains."

Celeste swallowed. "How do you know that?"

"I don't," the woman said gently. "The cards do. I only listen."

She gathered the deck, shuffling with the grace of ritual. "You'll dream again. Pay attention."

Celeste stood, the warmth of the tent suddenly stifling. "Thank you."

Outside, Lucie raised an eyebrow. "So? Am I to call you Madame Dufour, High Priestess of Saint-Marguerite?"

Celeste smiled, but faintly. "No. But maybe… maybe someday."

Lucie looked at her. "You're serious."

"Maybe."

They walked on, but the music and laughter felt distant now, as though the fair belonged to another world—and Celeste had just stepped out of it.

The fair was still echoing behind her when Celeste slipped away from the road and cut down toward the river path. Her boots crunched against frostbitten leaves, and the hem of her skirt snagged on wild branches, but she didn't care.

The Saint Lawrence lay ahead, vast and pewter-blue under a sky that couldn't decide whether to snow or sleep. A line of geese crossed in the distance, honking like old men in an argument.

She reached the shore and stood still.

The tarot cards floated behind her eyes—*The Tower, The High Priestess, The Star.* Even now, she couldn't recall their exact placement on the cloth. Only the feeling they had stirred, like wind under a locked door.

She drew the indigo book from her coat pocket. She hadn't dared read it at the fair, but now she opened to a random page.

"Ne cours pas vers l'éveil. Il viendra quand ton silence sera assez vaste pour l'entendre." (*Do not rush toward awakening. It will come when your silence is wide enough to hear it.*)

The wind picked up, swirling the hem of her coat and tugging at her scarf like a child.

She closed the book and pressed it to her chest.

Across the water, the cathedral bell rang—not from the belfry, but in her memory. A single, low note.

Her breath clouded the air. Her heartbeat slowed.

She felt—just for a moment—as though she were standing in two places at once. On the bank of the river, and inside it. Inside something much older than language, deeper than her family name, vaster than the geography of this town.

She didn't understand it.

But she didn't want to forget it.

The Cathedral of the Immaculate Conception rose like a fortress of certainty, its limestone towers clawing at the November sky. The bells rang out as always—commanding, proud—and Celeste followed her mother up the worn stone steps, her gloved hands clenched in her coat pockets.

Inside, the smell of incense and wax hit her like memory. She had been coming here since before she could read, before she even knew her own name meant *heavenly*. It was supposed to feel like coming home.

But it didn't.

They took their usual pew, fourth from the front on the left-hand side, beneath the stained-glass window of Saint Thérèse. Celeste used to love that window. The colours would dance on the stone floor when the sun hit them just right, like heaven itself had spilled through the glass.

Today, they just looked like coloured shadows.

Father Brousseau mounted the pulpit and cleared his throat.

"*Mes frères et sœurs,*" he began, voice slow and sure. "*Today, let us consider the importance of obedience. Obedience to the Church, to our families, to God's divine plan—even when we do not understand it.*"

Celeste felt her chest tighten.

She looked at her mother beside her—eyes closed, lips moving in rhythm with the priest's cadence. Around them, heads nodded, rosaries clicked, knees bent and straightened like the gears of a well-oiled machine.

But Celeste could not move.

A passage from the indigo book whispered in her memory: *"Obedience is not the same as truth. One can follow a path in silence and still be lost."*

Her pulse thudded in her ears. The pillars loomed higher than she remembered. The vaulted ceiling no longer reached upward—it pressed down.

She glanced toward the altar. The crucifix hung as always, Christ frozen in agony, but for the first time, she noticed something else: the way the candlelight flickered just behind his head. As though a flame were burning where none should be.

The rest of the service passed like a dream in reverse—familiar words she couldn't seem to enter, hymns she no longer wanted to sing.

When it was over, her mother rose and crossed herself with calm precision.

Celeste stayed seated for a moment longer.

Outside, the bells rang again. But this time, they didn't feel like a call.

They felt like a warning.

It began with the smell.

Celeste came home from school to the unmistakable scent of something charred. Not food. Not wood.

Paper.

Her heart stuttered. She dropped her satchel and ran for the stairs, taking them two at a time. Her bedroom door was open.

And on the floor, still smouldering in her mother's enamel basin, were the blackened remains of the indigo book.

Her mother stood over it, arms crossed, rosary wound tight around one hand like a weapon.

"What is this filth?" she hissed.

Celeste stopped in the doorway, breath caught in her throat.

"You went through my drawer."

"I clean your room every Thursday. This week, God told me to check deeper."

She jabbed a finger toward the basin. "Blasphemy. Occult symbols. *Witchcraft.* Have you completely lost your mind?"

"It's not witchcraft—"

"It's not *Catholic,*" her mother snapped. "And that is all that matters."

Celeste stepped forward. "It's not evil, Maman. It speaks of the soul. Of listening. Of finding truth."

"Truth?" Her mother's voice cracked. "You think truth comes from a book scribbled by some madwoman? You think I didn't notice the way you've changed? The silence at mass. The way you drift off in the middle of supper. What else have you been hiding from me?"

Celeste's fists clenched at her sides. "Myself."

Silence fell like an axe.

Her mother turned back to the basin, trembling. "I have lost one son to the war, another to silence, and a husband to the sea. I will not lose my daughter to fantasy."

She reached into the basin with the poker, stirring the ashes—but something stopped her.

A single page remained intact.

Celeste stepped forward and lifted it out. The edges were singed, but the centre was untouched. Her eyes locked on the words:

"Le feu peut éclairer ou consumer. Ce que tu tiens entre tes mains décidera." (Fire can illuminate or consume. What you hold in your hands will decide.)

Her mother crossed herself. "Even the devil quotes Scripture."

Celeste didn't answer. She folded the page carefully, cradling it like something living.

Without another word, she walked out of the room.

The sky was the colour of unwashed linen, streaked with late-afternoon gold. Celeste walked alone, the chill of November seeping through her coat, her boots whispering against the gravel path that led down to the river.

She carried only the single unburnt page, folded twice and tucked into her prayer book, where the pressed maple leaf still lived—its colour faded but intact.

The Saint Lawrence lay ahead, grey and endless.

She stepped onto the shore, where the river widened into the illusion of stillness. Ice had begun to gather at the edges in lace-like fractals. The wind stirred her hair, lifting it gently, as if to remind her she was still rooted to the earth, even as something in her threatened to rise.

Celeste knelt.

Not in prayer—but in presence.

She closed her eyes. The sounds of the town faded: the distant train, the hum of car engines, the echo of schoolchildren's laughter. All of it slipped into silence, like the closing of a door.

And then—

A feeling.

It came not from outside her, but from the very space within her ribs.

A lightness.

Not joy, exactly. Not relief. It was something older, quieter. As though a weight she had carried her whole life—a weight she'd never thought to name—had simply let go.

She breathed in, and the air tasted different. Clean. True.

Her mind stilled. Her hands relaxed. Her heart moved in rhythm with the river.

And for the first time, she did not feel alone.

She stood, slowly, as if waking from a sleep she hadn't known she'd fallen into. The river shimmered before her, vast and waiting. Not to be crossed. Not to be conquered.

Only to be heard.

Celeste placed the folded page back in her book. She touched the maple leaf once more, then turned away from the riverbank, her shadow long behind her.

She didn't know exactly where the path ahead would lead.

But she knew now that it was hers.

Two days later, Celeste found herself walking down Rue Saint-Louis again, boots echoing softly against the cobblestones. The fair was long gone. The sky had paled into winter's edge, and shop windows had begun to fill with tinselled saints and Christmas oranges.

She turned the familiar corner, heart tapping a quiet rhythm, and looked for the little shop.

It was gone.

Where *Librairie d'Occasion – Livres rares et oubliés* had once stood, there was now nothing but a blank brick wall. Not boarded up. Not closed. Just… as if it had never been there.

Celeste stood for a long moment, scanning the empty space. The narrow alley still ran alongside it, the same old drainpipe clung to the bricks—but the window, the door, the faded sign… gone.

She let out a breath. Not disappointment. Not confusion.

Just awe.

Then, quietly, she smiled.

Because of course it was gone. Some doors only open once.

And only when you're ready to step through.

The windows stuck. No matter how he angled the screen or tugged the sash, Liam couldn't get it to stay open wider than a crack. Still, it let in enough breeze to stir the edge of the envelope on his kitchen table—just enough to make him look at it again.

Postmarked from home. Clara's tidy block letters. He hadn't opened it yet.

Outside, the street murmured with mid-October life: a delivery truck idling half on the curb, someone wheeling a bike up the sidewalk, the faint clatter of a windchime from the balcony above. The air was still warm—barefoot-on-linoleum warm—but with that dry, hollow sound to it. Like summer was leaving and taking all the softness with it.

From the kitchen window, Liam could just make out the top of a small ash tree across the street. Its leaves had gone bright yellow, sharp as buttercups against the clear blue sky. A glowing thing in a city that had started to fade.

The campus down the street pulsed with a low, restless rhythm: masked students moving in clumps, their laughter cautious, like they weren't sure if they were allowed to be happy yet. There was that back-to-school energy in the air—new pens, new routines, half-hearted optimism—but filtered through the tension of distancing signs and sanitizer stations. Fall 2021. The year everything was still uncertain.

Liam ran a hand through his hair, still damp from the shower. His hoodie clung a little at the shoulders. He'd slept too long. Again.

He crossed to the counter, filled the kettle, clicked it on. The tiny apartment always smelled like someone else's dinner. Today it was onions and cloves—maybe the neighbour downstairs was making biryani again.

He didn't mind. The noise, the closeness, even the occasional shouting through the walls—it reminded him he wasn't floating in space. That other lives were happening.

The envelope rustled again in the window draft.

Liam turned his back to it and opened the cupboard instead. Instant oatmeal. A few crackers. Peanut butter. Not much of a breakfast, but better than nothing.

His phone buzzed: a notification from the student LGBTQ group:

🗣️ Protest November 12! 12pm @ Front Campus.
Bring a sign + a mask.
Let's make some noise.

He stared at it, thumb hovering.

Make some noise.

Right. Like that ever helped.

He clicked the kettle off before it finished boiling and poured just enough into his mug.

Then, almost without thinking, he slid the envelope from Clara into his desk drawer and shut it.

Outside, the little ash tree flickered in the wind—yellow leaves catching the light like tiny flames, burning bright against the blue.

Friday, November 12. The kind of grey, bone-damp day Toronto did best. Wind like a wet sleeve against the skin, trees half-stripped of their leaves, the sidewalks slick with yesterday's rain. A few discarded plastic poppies lay crushed in the gutter, their red petals muddied under boot prints—leftovers from the day before.

Liam walked toward Front Campus with his mask already on and a folded cardboard sign under his arm. He hadn't written anything clever—just *"We deserve to be safe"* in thick block letters. The ink had bled slightly in the humidity.

The square was filling in fast. Chalk slogans blurred at the edges. Someone drummed on a plastic bucket, rhythm steady and low. There were students handing out rainbow ribbon pins, sanitizing their hands between each exchange. A few faculty stood at the edge in support, their body language somewhere between cautious and proud.

Liam kept to the periphery. Not because he was scared—he told himself—but because it was easier to observe than to occupy space. He wasn't used to being loud. Not yet.

And then he saw him.

Dark-haired. Tall. Standing still in a sea of movement, face hidden behind a solid black mask. His T-shirt was minimalist—black cotton, absurdly placed over a grey hoodie, with white block letters that read simply: **MATTER MATTERS.**

Liam almost didn't notice the sign at first. It was held close to the guy's chest, low, like he wasn't trying to be seen—but still wanted to be heard. *"Silence is the real contagion,"* it read, white paint on black bristol board. Stark. Direct.

Something in Liam's chest pinched and didn't let go.

They made eye contact for a second. The guy's eyes were a deep, unreadable colour—hazel maybe, or green-brown in that way that shifted depending on the light.

Liam looked away first, then back, just as the chant started near the front:

"No pride in silence! No pride in shame!"

He lifted his sign. Not high. Just enough.

He saw the dark-haired guy helping someone adjust their mic

stand, calm and competent. The kind of person who didn't need to take up space to shape it.

And then—without fanfare or hesitation—the guy looked up, met Liam's gaze again, and nodded. A small nod. Barely there.

Liam didn't smile. He didn't wave. But he felt something steady settle in his ribs.

He didn't know the guy's name. Didn't know if he was gay, bi, anything. Didn't know if he'd ever see him again.

But he knew that, for the first time in weeks, he didn't feel invisible.

And that was something.

Liam kicked off his boots just inside the door, the soles still damp from the sidewalk. He didn't bother with the overhead light—just let the city spill in through the cracked blinds, painting soft grids of amber across the kitchen tiles.

He peeled off his hoodie, dropped it over the back of the chair, and stood for a moment with his hands braced on the counter. The apartment smelled like cumin and toast. Probably the guy downstairs again. Or maybe it had just seeped into the walls by now.

The protest still buzzed in his ears—chant rhythms looping in the quiet, a phantom pressure behind his ribs where he'd been holding the sign. That ache again, not pain exactly. Just proof that he still wanted something.

He opened the fridge, stared into it without registering what was inside, then closed it again.

Slumped into the desk chair.

His phone was still in his pocket. He pulled it out. No messages. No updates. The protest had been anonymous like that—everyone hidden behind masks and hoods, names replaced by chants and slogans.

Except for him.

The guy in the **MATTER MATTERS** shirt. The one with the dark hair and quiet eyes and the sign that didn't ask for attention, just offered a truth.

Liam didn't know why that stuck.

He hadn't even said a word.

Still. There'd been something in the way he nodded. Like he'd seen him. Like he'd meant to.

Liam set the phone down face-first and let himself exhale.

He didn't believe in signs. Not really. But sometimes a look could open a door.

Sometimes all you needed was a reason to knock.

It came three days later. Another plain white envelope, slightly crumpled, with Clara's handwriting on the front—careful block letters like she was still trying to make every word teacher-perfect.

Liam found it wedged into the middle of the week's mail, sandwiched between a discount pizza flyer and a notice about flu shots. No return address, but the postmark said it all.

He didn't open it right away.

He tucked it into his hoodie pocket, where it stayed through the walk upstairs, through reheating a mug of day-old coffee, through scrolling half-heartedly on his phone.

It wasn't until the shadows stretched long across the living room floor that he finally unfolded the letter and sat down to read.

Hi Liam,

It's Clara. Obviously. I hope you're eating things besides cereal. I know you probably aren't, but I'm going to pretend you are.

School is okay. Mr. Jamal is still weird about decimals, but he likes my diorama. I made it out of shoeboxes and glitter glue. It's the Solar System. Pluto's in it anyway because it deserves better.

Mom doesn't say much. Dad's still Dad. But I thought you should know—

Liam's eyes caught the next line before his brain could brace for it.

Charlie died last week. He kept looking at the door like he thought you'd come back.

The words hit like ice water. No warning. No buildup. Just a cold snap to the chest.

He had to blink a few times before the rest of the letter came into focus.

I put one of your T-shirts in his bed. The soft one you used to wear when you watched cartoons with me. I think he liked it. Anyway, I miss you. And he did too. A lot.

I'm not mad at you. I get why you had to leave. I just hope someday we can watch dumb cartoons again, maybe with a new dog who likes the same snacks.

Love, Clara

P.S. Write back this time, you jerk.

Liam folded the letter carefully and pressed his palm over it, flat against the kitchen table. The vinyl surface was warm from the sun that had passed through earlier. His throat felt tight, like he'd swallowed something too big.

He wanted to call her. Immediately. But he knew he couldn't.

Not with the house lines still under Dad's thumb. Not with his number probably blocked.

Instead, he got up, went to his laptop, and changed the home screen.

The picture he picked was one from the spring before everything blew up—Charlie on the back deck, tongue lolling, fur all angles and joy.

He stared at it a long time. Then, quietly, with a catch in his voice, he whispered, "I'm sorry, buddy."

The ash tree outside had shed most of its leaves, but one still clung to the topmost branch. A flicker of yellow against the evening blue.

That night, the apartment felt too quiet.

Liam lay on his side on the couch, Clara's letter folded into his hands, the photo of Charlie glowing faintly from his laptop screen across the room.

He kept seeing it—Charlie turning toward the front door, tail thumping once, then still.

It wasn't just the dog. It was everything. The silence. The look on his mother's face when she didn't stop his father from shouting. The way no one ran after him when he left.

He hadn't cried that night. Or the next. He'd packed, kept moving, started over like it was something clean.

But now, in this dim kitchen-living-everything room, it caught up with him.

The ache swelled in his chest like a fault line finally giving way.

And he cried.

Quiet at first, like he didn't want to disturb the neighbours. Then louder. Shoulders shaking, hands curled into fists on the couch cushions.

It wasn't just for Charlie. It was for Clara, stuck in that house. For the dinners he wouldn't be invited to. For the way his father's voice still echoed in his memory, sharp and final.

He cried until the tears stopped coming, and the shaking gave way to stillness.

When he finally sat up, the letter was still in his hands. A little wrinkled now. Smudged near the bottom, where his thumb had been.

He smoothed it out, refolded it along the creases, and tucked it into the front of his journal.

Not hidden. Just held.

The sky was brittle blue, sun low and angled, shadows sharp across the paving stones. The wind had calmed for once, and Liam pulled his coat tighter, the collar tucked up against the chill.

He hadn't planned to walk back to the protest site. It just... happened. His feet brought him there, past the spot where the rainbow ribbons had been handed out, past the low wall where the loudest chants had echoed.

Now it was quiet. A few masked students crossing campus. Pigeons milling around an abandoned sandwich crust. The faint, fading traces of chalk slogans, softened by wind and weather.

Liam crouched beside a wall, the kind that had once bristled with signs and posters. In the quiet, he pulled a stick of white chalk from his pocket and wrote, in careful block letters:

STILL HERE.

The chalk stuttered as it caught in the stone's texture. He went over the lines again, making them solid. Present.

A voice behind him said, "Good choice."

Liam turned slightly.

It was him.

MATTER MATTERS.

Same dark hair, tousled beneath a green toque. Black mask. Canvas jacket with physics buttons down one lapel, and—yes—Schrödinger's cat curled into the fold of his sleeve.

Up close, his eyes were flecked green and gold, unreadable and clear at once.

"I mean," the guy added, nodding toward the chalk, "we are. Still here. Doesn't always feel like it, but..."

He trailed off with a shrug.

Liam nodded. "Yeah. I know what you mean."

The guy pulled something from his coat pocket: a pack of chalks in rainbow colours. "In case you wanna add colour."

"Thanks," Liam said, a little surprised.

"I'm Rowan," the guy offered, voice lower now, like they'd stepped into a different kind of quiet.

"Liam."

They stood a beat, tension dissolving slightly in the rhythm of breath and ambient birdsong.

"Your shirt the other day," Liam said, "simple, but solid."

Rowan's eyes crinkled. "I'm a minimalist with a message."

Liam gave a short laugh. "Physics branding?"

"More or less." Rowan crouched beside him, pulled out a pale blue chalk, and wrote beneath Liam's words:

PUSH YOURSELF A LITTLE FURTHER THAN YOU DARE.

Liam read it twice. Something about the way it sloped upward at the end made it feel like a rising note.

"That's good," he said. "Yours?"

Rowan shook his head. "Audre Lorde."

"Good choice," Liam echoed.

Rowan wiped his fingers on his coat. "We need reminders sometimes."

They crouched there a moment longer, chalk dust between them, the quiet not uncomfortable.

Liam didn't say anything else. Not yet. But something had changed.

The silence didn't feel empty anymore.

Later that evening, Liam sat cross-legged on the floor with a chipped mug of mint tea and his journal open in front of him. The only light came from the desk lamp behind him, casting warm gold across the pages.

He hadn't written anything yet. The pen rested beside his knee, untouched.

He kept thinking about Rowan's eyes.

Not in a dramatic, hearts-and-stars kind of way—just in that quiet, persistent way something stays with you when it matters more than you realize.

Push yourself a little further than you dare.

He didn't know what he'd expected from that walk back to the protest site. Closure, maybe. Some kind of symbolic release. Not Rowan. Not chalk quotes and rainbow dust and the briefest hum of something like trust.

Liam turned to a fresh page in the journal and, without planning it, copied the quote down.

He underlined *dare* twice.

His phone buzzed with a news alert. He ignored it.

Then, on impulse, he opened his messages. No new ones from Clara. Nothing from his parents, of course. Just a handful of old conversations and a few unanswered invites to digital mixers he hadn't felt brave enough to attend.

He didn't know if Rowan would be at the next protest.

Didn't know if he even *went* to mixers.

But now he knew his name. And that was something.

The café on Bloor wasn't one of the sleek ones with neon signage or industrial lightbulbs in birdcage fixtures. It was older, a little faded, with a bulletin board covered in yellowing flyers and a staff that didn't flinch at mismatched mugs or overlong laptop stays.

Liam liked it because it didn't pretend to be more than it was. And the coffee was good.

He was halfway through a lemon poppyseed muffin when Rowan walked in—shoulders hunched slightly from the cold, toque shoved in his coat pocket. His hair stuck up a bit in the back, like he'd forgotten to check a mirror before leaving the house.

Liam waved him over.

"Sorry I'm late," Rowan said, sliding into the booth across from him. "I got quantum-looped in the physics building."

Liam raised an eyebrow. "That a technical term?"

Rowan grinned. "It is now."

They sipped their drinks in companionable quiet for a moment. Outside, the street glinted wet under a rare burst of sun, the kind of light that made the concrete look almost silver.

"I wasn't sure you'd come," Liam said, not quite looking at him.

"Me neither," Rowan admitted. "But... you wrote *Still here.* And I guess I wanted to be."

Liam let out a breath he hadn't realised he was holding.

They talked after that. Not about anything huge—weather, assignments, a professor Rowan mimicked with uncanny precision that made Liam laugh so hard he snorted into his tea.

Eventually, the edges softened enough for something real to slip through.

Rowan fiddled with the cardboard sleeve on his cup. "You mentioned... the other day, about not getting the choice? With your family?"

Liam hesitated, then nodded. "They found out. My dad... didn't take it well. My mom let him say what he needed to say, which was almost worse."

"I'm sorry," Rowan said, and he meant it. No qualifiers. No awkward follow-up.

"It's okay," Liam said quietly. "I mean, it's not. But it's real."

Rowan picked at the seam of the cup. "I'm not out. Not to them. I don't even know what they'd say, honestly. Probably... nothing. And that scares me."

There was a long pause.

Then Rowan added, in a voice just loud enough to carry: "You strike a chord, man. And I can't have that chord struck. Not yet."

Liam looked at him then. Really looked.

"I get that," he said. "I just... don't want to be music you can't play."

Rowan didn't answer right away. But his gaze held, steady and unreadable.

Outside, a breeze lifted the edge of a discarded napkin on the patio table, and the sun—unexpected, defiant—broke through the clouds one last time before disappearing again.

That evening, Liam sat on the windowsill in his apartment, mug of reheated tea warming his hands. The sky had gone that deep indigo-grey Toronto did so well—cloud cover thick, with the streetlights already fuzzing halos through the mist.

He pulled out his phone and opened his messages. Clara's name sat there in its usual place, the last thread he hadn't let unravel.

No response yet to the letter he hadn't written. But she'd reached out first. Maybe that was enough.

His thumbs hovered for a moment, then typed:

Hey, Clara. I miss you too. And I'm sorry about Charlie. I put his photo as my laptop background—he's still here, in a way.

I met someone. Not *like that*, not yet. Just someone who makes me feel... less alone.

Anyway. I hope Pluto got an A. Your diorama sounds way cooler than mine was.

He stared at the message for a few seconds, then added:

Love you, spacemonkey.

—L

He hit send.

The little status bar flicked across. Delivered.

Outside, the wind picked up again, leaves scraping across the sidewalk like soft applause.

It was a Wednesday, the kind that pretended to be colder than it was—more wind than weather. Liam had just finished tutoring a first-year student who didn't know how commas worked when he spotted Rowan standing outside the café with two takeaway cups and a brown paper bag.

Rowan waved one cup in the air. "You looked like a man in need of sugar and caffeine."

Liam stepped closer. "You're not wrong."

They took their drinks to a nearby bench, one sheltered by the skeleton of what used to be a leafy maple. Most of the leaves had dropped now—dry, curled things skittering across the concrete like lost notes.

Rowan was wearing a black T-shirt under his flannel jacket, just visible where it peeked open at the chest. The shirt featured a stovetop with four coils, an ohm symbol in the middle, and a caption beneath:
OHM ON THE RANGE

Liam snorted. "Really?"

Rowan looked down. "You like?"

"It's aggressively physics. But I'll allow it."

Rowan grinned, then pulled a slim, dog-eared book from his satchel and handed it over without fanfare.

Liam took it carefully. The title gleamed faintly under the streetlight: *The Tao of Physics.*

"You mentioned once," Rowan said, "that you still believe. In something. I don't really know what I believe yet. But this made me think about it differently."

Liam opened the cover. Inside, written in neat, small letters:

For the boy who believes in things that can't be seen.

He blinked a few times. Shut the book. Looked at Rowan.

"You didn't have to..."

"I know," Rowan said quickly. "It's not—like—a declaration or anything. Just... something that helped me connect dots. Maybe it'll do that for you too."

Liam nodded slowly, turning the book over in his hands.

"This means a lot," he said.

Rowan gave a one-shouldered shrug, but there was colour rising in his face just above the mask line.

They sat quietly for a while, sipping warm drinks as the sky turned violet and the streetlights blinked into life.

Liam thought about quantum entanglement, about how two particles could remain connected no matter the distance between them.

And how, in the most parallel of universes, people could too.

The texts stopped first.

Not abruptly—just a quiet drift into silence. A meme left on read. A question about Thursday's protest never answered.

Liam waited two days before convincing himself not to overreact. Then a third. By day four, the silence had weight.

It wasn't that he needed Rowan to say anything big. Just... *anything*.

He scrolled through their thread at night, re-reading the short bursts of banter, the quote from Lorde, a blurry picture Rowan had sent of a double rainbow over Robarts Library with the caption: *This city gets dramatic sometimes.*

Now it was just blank space. The absence of reply made each previous message echo harder.

Liam found himself rereading the inscription in the book. Over and over.

For the boy who believes in things that can't be seen.

So what was he now?

He didn't reach out again. Not yet. If Rowan had needed space, fine. Liam could give it.

He'd given space before. Whole canyons of it.

But damn, it still hurt.

It was the second week of January. That stretch of winter where everything felt like a reset you hadn't asked for.

Liam was walking along College Street, boots crunching in old snow, the sky that dull, unchangeable slate Toronto wore for weeks at a time. The sidewalks were lined with frozen mud, piled at sharp angles, like failed attempts at clearing things away.

Coffeeshop windows glowed weakly through condensation. Inside, people clutched paper cups and leaned over laptops, their faces lit by the soft blue of screens and overhead fluorescents.

He nearly didn't see Rowan until they were almost level—standing at the corner beneath a bare-branched tree, bundled in his coat and green toque, no mask this time.

"Hey," Rowan said, his voice soft but unmistakable.

Liam stopped. The cold wrapped around them like insulation.

Rowan looked tired. Not in a dramatic way, just worn at the edges. Hollow-eyed and real.

"My parents called. Back in December," he said. "Asking when I was coming home for the holidays."

Liam nodded slowly. "You didn't go?"

"No." A pause. "Said I had too much work. Wasn't really true. But they didn't press."

He looked down at the icy sidewalk, then back up.

"I didn't mean to disappear. I just—needed to figure out if I could stand still without falling apart."

Liam said nothing. Let the words settle.

"You scare me," Rowan added, almost a whisper. "Because you're… there. You listen. You care. And I didn't know how to hold that without dropping it."

Liam's breath clouded in the air between them.

"I'm not perfect at this," Rowan said. "I'm trying."

Liam looked at him fully. "You left without a word. After giving me that book. After everything."

"I know." Rowan's eyes didn't flinch. "But I've thought about you every day since. And the truth is… I'd rather hear the music than keep plugging my ears."

Liam gave a half-laugh, half-sigh. "You're still going with the music metaphor?"

Rowan smiled faintly. "I'm a physics major. We don't get a lot of poetry."

A beat passed.

Then Liam said, "Just... don't disappear again. If you need space, tell me. But don't leave me trying to read silence."

"I won't," Rowan said. "I'm still here."

They didn't touch. But something cracked open, soft and clean, like the sound of ice breaking on the lake.

For the first time in a long while, the cold didn't feel so lonely.

It was the kind of night that held its breath.

The wind had stilled for once, and the snowflakes that lingered in the air fell soft and slow, like they were reluctant to land.

Liam and Rowan sat on the rooftop of Liam's building, knees drawn up, a thick blanket shared between them. Their breath rose in twin plumes as they passed a thermos of hot chocolate back and forth.

Below them, the city hummed—low traffic, distant music, a train horn miles away. Lights glimmered in scattered windows, tiny declarations that people were still awake, still making it through.

Rowan nudged Liam gently with his shoulder. "You ever think about how ridiculous it is that we're here?"

Liam raised an eyebrow. "Here as in Toronto, or here as in... under a blanket on my roof?"

"Both. And also, like, here. Alive. Together. At all."

Liam let out a quiet breath. "Yeah. A lot, actually."

There was a pause, the good kind.

"I still don't know what I believe," Rowan said. "About fate, or parallel universes, or anything like that."

Liam looked up. The stars were faint, but they were there.

"I do," he said. "A little."

Rowan glanced over. "Yeah?"

Liam pulled out his phone and showed him the home screen—a photo of Charlie on the back deck, tongue out, eyes bright.

Rowan smiled, soft and full of knowing. "Good boy."

Liam nodded. "Yeah. The best."

He tucked the phone away, then looked at Rowan. "You're not just striking a chord, you know."

Rowan tilted his head. "No?"

"You're changing the key."

Rowan let that settle between them.

"Then," he said, voice steady, "let's write a new song."

They didn't kiss—not yet.

But they leaned into each other, the blanket wrapped around them like a held breath. And as snow fell softly onto the rooftop gravel, Liam let himself believe—not in forever, but in this.

This moment. This connection. This second chance.

And that was enough. For now.

"Is fusa cuimhne a chothú ná dearmad."
It is easier to remember than to forget.

The kettle whistled in the cramped kitchen, a thin scream above the drone of the evening news. Tobias hunched over the battered table, picking at the frayed seam of his jumper sleeve, pretending not to hear his father's grumbled curses from the sitting room.

"Talk of peace," the man spat, the chair legs scraping violently against the worn floorboards. "As if a handshake could wash the blood from their hands."

Tobias didn't know who *they* were this time. It changed, depending on the headlines. Catholics, Protestants, politicians, peacemakers—it hardly seemed to matter. All he knew was that the air in the house got heavier when his father's voice rose, thickening like the mist that rolled down from the hills at night.

At the stove, his grandmother stirred the tea with steady hands, her silver hair pulled tight at the nape of her neck. She said nothing. She rarely did, not when anger prowled the house like a dog with nowhere to go.

Without looking at Tobias, she slid a battered tin into his hands—two loaves of soda bread inside, still warm from the oven.

"Take these to Mrs. Kavanagh," she said, her voice low and even. "And take the long way, a stór. Past the fields."

Tobias met her eyes for a fraction of a second—grey like stormlight, full of things she would not say in front of his father. He understood. He always understood.

He shoved the tin under his arm and slipped on his too-large boots, the ones his father had scowled at but grudgingly accepted because they were cheap.

"Don't dawdle," his father barked from the other room, though he never looked up.

Tobias pulled the door shut behind him, the latch catching with a tired clunk.

The chill outside bit at his cheeks. He welcomed it. The sky stretched low and bruised above him, the hedgerows brittle and skeletal against the fading light.

He could have taken the lane into the village. Could have walked along the cracked pavement past Mr. Doyle's feed store and the silent post office. Could have done what was expected.

Instead, Tobias turned his boots toward the fields.

The long way.

The way that waited.

"Féach thart ort."

Look around you.

The fields opened before him, wide and wild, stitched with low stone walls and the last stubborn scraps of mist. Each step away from the house lightened something tight in Tobias's chest, as if the air itself grew easier to breathe once he crossed the edge of his father's domain.

The tin was warm against his ribs. Mrs. Kavanagh's cottage was a good half-hour away this way—maybe longer if he lost himself. Tobias didn't mind.

He veered off the narrow lane, boots squelching over the damp earth. Grass brushed his shins, heavy with clinging drops of yesterday's rain. Somewhere in the distance, a crow cried out, its voice harsh against the soft hush of the landscape.

Past the first hedgerow stood an old wall—its stones blackened by rain, softened by moss, and split by the careless carving of boys' names long forgotten. Near the base, faded by time and lichen, a patch of political slogans bled through:

"Tiocfaidh ár lá."

"No surrender."

Old war cries. New graffiti scrawled over the old.

Tobias slowed, tracing the ghost of a handprint on the stone.

He didn't really remember his mother. Not her laugh, not her stories. Only a flash of red—her scarf, maybe—floating behind a pram in a summer breeze. His grandmother said she'd been caught in the wrong place on the wrong day. A market bombing. She hadn't even been political.

None of it made sense to Tobias. None of it ever would.

The tin shifted under his arm. He shook himself and pressed on.

The land sloped upward here, and the mist thickened. The sun, low and watery behind the clouds, gilded the horizon in tarnished silver.

That was when he saw it.

The fox.

It stood at the top of the rise, poised as if stitched into the fading light. Its coat was a deep copper, darker than any Tobias had seen, its brush of a tail tipped in black. It looked straight at him—not skittish, not wild.

Knowing.

Tobias froze.

The fox didn't bolt. Instead, it dipped its head once, almost like a bow, and turned—padding silently toward the shadowed line of trees at the field's edge.

Without thinking, Tobias followed.

His boots crunched over frost-tipped grass. He half-forgot the tin tucked against his side. He half-forgot Mrs. Kavanagh. All he could see was the place where the trees thickened, where the mist clung close to the earth like something breathing.

The fox slipped between two gnarled trunks and disappeared.

Tobias hesitated at the threshold. The oaks loomed, ancient and skeletal, their bare branches netted high against the dimming sky. The air tasted different here—earthier, sharper, threaded with the scent of damp bark and something older still.

He swallowed.

The wind stirred the leaves at his feet, carrying a whisper he almost thought he could understand:

"Féach thart ort."

Look around you.

He stepped into the grove.

"Tá tú ag filleadh."

You are returning.

The grove closed around him like a held breath.

The moment Tobias stepped past the first line of trees, the air shifted. The sounds of the outer world—crows, distant cars, even the wind—muffled into stillness. All that remained was the soft crunch of leaf-litter beneath his boots and the hush of something unseen watching gently.

The trees here were older. Massive oaks, their trunks twisted like sleeping giants, roots like knuckled hands grasping deep into the earth. Moss clung to everything—green-gold and softly glowing in the dim light.

And something else.

Stone.

Tobias crouched beside a flat rock partially buried beneath the undergrowth. It bore a carved pattern, half-erased by time. A circle knotted into itself. No beginning, no end.

A Celtic knot.

He ran his fingers over the grooves, half expecting the stone to breathe. His grandmother had once told him these knots were maps for the soul. "You can get lost in one," she'd said, "but that's how you find your way back."

Something flitted just at the edge of his sight—a flicker of white cloth, or maybe just mist. He stood, heart thudding, and turned slowly.

There, standing beneath the largest oak, was a figure.

A man.

He looked as though he'd stepped out of the stones themselves: cloaked in grey that shimmered like bark, a staff in one hand, the other outstretched as if in welcome. His beard was streaked with silver, his eyes unreadable but kind. They met Tobias's gaze and did not waver.

Tobias couldn't speak.

The man did not smile, but there was warmth in his voice when he finally spoke.

"You've come far, little one."

His accent was lilting, Irish but older somehow, as though shaped by forest and time.

"I didn't mean to," Tobias whispered.

"Most never do." The man tilted his head. "But still, they come."

He stepped forward, the leaves whispering under his feet.

"Do you know where you are?"

Tobias shook his head.

The man pointed with the tip of his staff to the largest tree, where another knot—much deeper, much older—was carved into the bark.

"This place remembers," he said softly. "Even when people forget."

Tobias's hand drifted to his chest without thinking, as though the stone knot from the clearing were now lodged beneath his ribs.

The man seemed to notice. "You feel it, don't you? The old blood. The knowing."

"I don't know anything," Tobias said.

At that, the man gave a small, rustling laugh, like leaves stirring. "You know more than most grown men I've met."

He reached into the folds of his cloak and drew out something small: a pendant, carved from dark wood, shaped in a familiar knot.

He held it out.

Tobias didn't move.

"For me?"

"No," the man said. "For the boy who listens. For the one who remembers what others choose to forget."

Tobias stepped forward and took it. The wood was warm, impossibly so, as though it had been carved from something still living.

"What do I do with it?" he asked.

The man's voice dropped to something almost like prayer.

"Ná déan dearmad."

Do not forget.

Tobias clutched the knot in his hand, heart beating loud in the stillness.

Then the man raised a hand—and the trees began to shift, not in space but in time.

Light fractured around them.

For one impossible moment, Tobias saw the grove as it had been centuries before: people gathered in a wide circle, fire flickering in the centre, their faces turned upward in reverence. Children danced with garlands of oak leaves, old women chanted in a tongue he couldn't follow but somehow understood.

A different kind of Ireland. One not defined by war.

Then it was gone.

The fire, the dancers, the light—all vanished like breath on glass.

Only the trees remained.

And the man.

But even he was fading now—into the grey, into the bark, into the knotwork of the world.

"You're part of it now," the Druid said softly. "Be steady."

Then: silence.

Only the rustle of leaves.

Only Tobias.

Alone.

Except—not.

He tucked the pendant into his shirt and turned toward the edge of the grove.

The world waited beyond.

"Ná déan dearmad."

Do not forget.

The light had changed.

When Tobias stepped out of the grove, the sky was tinged with ash, the last breath of day slipping beneath the hills. The field felt flatter now. Smaller. As though the trees behind him had stretched time in a way the world couldn't measure.

He looked back once.

The grove stood still, patient as ever, revealing nothing. No trace of the man in grey. No fox. Only oaks, old as memory.

Tobias drew in a slow breath, the knot pendant warm beneath his shirt. He let his hand rest over it, fingers splayed, as if to anchor something that might otherwise fly away.

Then he walked.

The mud clung more this time. The grass felt less golden. But Tobias didn't mind. The world was as it had been, and yet... not.

The village lights blinked on in the distance as he neared the edge of the fields. His boots squelched up the lane, past the mural wall. He paused there.

Someone had scrawled a curse over the old painted slogans. Another name added to the list. Another wound layered over a wound. Tobias stared for a moment, then moved on.

He found Mrs. Kavanagh at her kitchen table, radio on, knitting needles dancing between gnarled fingers. She blinked at the bread tin, surprised but grateful.

"Yer grandmother makes the best soda bread this side of Armagh," she said, touching Tobias's cheek briefly with a soft, liver-spotted hand. "Tell her I said so."

He nodded. Didn't say much. Couldn't have, even if he'd tried.

The walk home was shorter than before. Somehow.

He saw the porch light flicker as he came around the bend. The front door creaked open just as he reached the step.

His father stood in the frame, one hand on the doorknob, the other holding a half-drained glass of something dark.

"Where've you been?" The voice wasn't angry, not quite. But it carried a tension, the kind that lived in a man who didn't know how to name fear except in the shape of blame.

"Went the long way," Tobias said.

His father's eyes narrowed. "Off dreaming, were you? That forest'll make a fool of you. Full of ghosts and stories."

Tobias said nothing.

The man grunted and stepped aside.

"Next time, come back sooner. Bread's not worth freezing for."

Tobias stepped into the warmth. Closed the door.

His grandmother looked up from the stove, nodded once, knowingly, and turned back to her pot.

Upstairs, the little room with the sloped ceiling and single bed welcomed him like an old friend. He took off his boots, lined them up neatly, and sat on the edge of the mattress.

Only then did he take the pendant from beneath his shirt.

The light of the hallway caught on its carved edges—the knot looping into itself, infinite, eternal.

He set it on the bedside table. Just for now.

Then lay back, hands folded behind his head, eyes on the patch of stars just visible through the slanted pane of glass.

The house creaked. The wind breathed against the eaves.

In his chest, the weight of the knot remained—not heavy, not strange.

Just *true*.

He closed his eyes.

And remembered.

The rain had started at lunch hour, hammering the school windows with a desperate kind of rhythm, and by the time Grace stumbled home, her shoes were soaked through and her backpack was leaking a trail of water across the floor. She slammed the door harder than she meant to, the hollow thud echoing through the small apartment.

She dropped her bag at the door and peeled off her wet jacket, tossing it over the banister. Her skin felt clammy, her throat sore from holding back tears. Not real tears—not yet—just that awful sting that clogged her nose and made her chest too tight to breathe properly.

Behind her eyes, the scene played again: the note in her locker, written in a messy scrawl she had convinced herself was authentic. *Meet me behind the gym after lunch. I like you.* A heart drawn underneath.

She'd believed it.

She'd hoped—stupidly, achingly—that Mark Langley, with his sun-bleached hair and soccer captain grin, might have seen something special in her. Something more than the too-big nose and the quiet bookishness.

Instead, she'd walked straight into a trap. A few boys loitering there, waiting for the punchline. Mark himself—red-faced, laughing too loudly—sputtering, "As if I'd ever like her."

And Grace, caught blinking in the rain, her heart cracking open like thin ice underfoot.

She wandered through the apartment now, trailing wet sock prints behind her, not caring. The house smelled like dust and bergamot—the remnants of Rivka's morning tea. It was quiet except for the tick of the old clock and the low whisper of the rain against the windows.

Her feet led her without thinking toward Rivka's bedroom. She knew she shouldn't. Rivka's room was private, a museum of old-world things that didn't like to be touched. But today, the air felt... different. Looser. As if the house itself had turned a blind eye.

The mirror caught her first.

It sat atop Rivka's dresser—a heavy oval in a dark wood frame, its silvered surface slightly warped at the edges. Grace had seen it a hundred times, but today it seemed to lean toward her. As if it had been waiting.

She stepped closer.

Her reflection swam into view: soaked hair clinging to her cheeks, the bridge of her nose reddened from the cold. The same face she'd seen all her life, but now it looked somehow foreign. Too sharp. Too unfinished.

Grace reached out and laid her fingertips lightly against the glass.

The room blurred.

The dresser, the rain, the apartment—they melted away. In their place: stone walls, heavy with the dust of another century. The air smelled of sun-baked earth and smoke. And in the mirror, standing where Grace should have been, was another girl.

Older—maybe thirteen, maybe fourteen. Dark hair plaited neatly down her back. A simple linen dress brushing her ankles. Her eyes—oh, her eyes—were Grace's own, but carrying a weight she didn't recognize. A knowing.

The girl lifted her hand, mirroring Grace's. For a moment their palms nearly touched, separated only by a breath of glass.

A whisper stirred the air, so soft Grace couldn't catch the words. Not English—something older, rounder at the edges. Familiar and unreachable all at once.

Grace stumbled back.

Her hip knocked against the dresser, sending a small porcelain perfume bottle clattering to the floor. The sharp scent of violets filled the air.

When she looked again, the mirror held only her own reflection—wide-eyed, pale, the apartment walls solid once more behind her. The rain resumed its soft drumming against the windows, as if nothing had happened at all.

She backed away from the dresser, her breath hitching in her chest, and fled to the living room. She curled into the corner of the sofa, drawing her knees tight against her chest, and stared blankly at the grey light leaking through the curtains.

It was there that Rivka found her.

The older woman said nothing at first, just set down her shopping bags and crossed the room with slow, sure steps. She lowered herself onto the sofa beside Grace, her movements careful, her presence as steady as stone.

Grace didn't speak. She didn't know how to.

Rivka rested a hand lightly on her granddaughter's damp hair, smoothing it back from her forehead. "Hard day?"

Grace gave the smallest nod.

They sat like that for a while, the old clock marking time in patient beats.

Finally, Grace whispered, "I think I saw... someone. In your mirror."

Rivka's hand stilled for a moment, then resumed its gentle path.

"Zofia's mirror," she said softly. "It belonged to my sister."

Grace turned her face toward her. "Was it… her?"

Rivka's eyes, deep and dark as turned soil, met hers. "Maybe. Or maybe it was someone you carry inside you."

Grace frowned, confused.

Rivka's voice dropped to a murmur, as if sharing a secret meant only for the rain and the dust and the blood that linked them. "There are memories written in flesh, Grace. Not all memory lives in the mind."

She pressed a kiss to Grace's forehead, her lips cool and dry.

"Sometimes," Rivka said, "we remember who we are by glimpsing who we have been."

Grace closed her eyes, the words settling over her like a quilt. She didn't understand. Not really. But something in her—something deep and old and bruised—knew it was true.

Outside, the rain softened to a mist, and the heavy clouds began to lift, just enough to let a sliver of light through.

The mirror waited in the darkened bedroom, holding its secrets. But Grace was not afraid.

Not anymore.

Rivka's Piano

The apartment smelled of warm challah and rising dusk.

Rachel Cohen sat at the battered upright piano, legs swinging a few inches above the floor, her small fingers stiff over the keys. The sheet music — a simple arrangement of *Eliyahu Hanavi* — drooped on the stand, curling at the corners like it wanted to give up too.

She stumbled again. A wrong note, a fumbling restart. The piano clanged in protest.

From the tiny kitchen, Rivka's voice floated out, warm and steady: "You are doing fine, motek. Keep going."

Rachel gritted her teeth. "I can't," she said, more to the keys than to the air. Her hands balled into fists. The frustration boiled up, sharp and hot. She slammed her fists onto the keyboard, a jarring, broken chord.

Silence fell. Only the smell of baking bread and the ticking of the kitchen clock filled it.

A moment later, Rivka appeared in the doorway, wiping her hands on a flour-dusted towel. Her hair, silver and neatly pinned, had come loose at one temple. The lines on her face deepened as she knelt quietly beside Rachel.

“No one is born knowing,” she said gently. She placed her warm hand over Rachel’s clenched ones. “You think you must break yourself to be good. But that is not why we make music, kelech.”

Rachel blinked up at her, tears threatening but not yet fallen.

“Then why?” she whispered.

Rivka smiled — a tired, beautiful thing — and tilted her head toward the waiting piano. “For the ones who could not. For the ones who still can.”

Without waiting, Rivka pressed a single key — a soft, low note, imperfect and true.

"You see?" she said. "One note. Enough to begin."

Rachel’s hands unclenched. Slowly, she touched a key two octaves higher — a tentative echo.

Rivka smiled and nodded. "Good. Again."

Together, they stitched a fragile melody from the old song — Rivka anchoring the bass notes, Rachel chasing the higher ones, sometimes missing, sometimes landing just right. It wasn't polished. It wasn't concert hall music. It was something better: alive.

When they finished the melody, Rachel let out a shaky laugh, part relief and part wonder.

"I made so many mistakes," she said.

"You made music," Rivka answered, her fingers still resting lightly on the keys. She turned her hand over, palm up, and rested it against the piano’s worn side.

"This piano," she said quietly, "once belonged to my cousin Miriam."

Rachel tilted her head, sensing a story under the words.

"She was older than me — almost grown when I was still learning my letters. We lived in Nowa Góra, a little village with fields and stone houses, not much else. Her family was not rich, but they saved for this piano. It filled their house with music when nothing else could."

Rivka's thumb brushed an invisible line across the wood.

"When the soldiers came, I was only a little girl. Miriam was already a woman, brave enough to carry her music books with her when they herded us away. She thought..." Rivka's voice caught for a moment. "She thought if she played, maybe they would listen. Maybe they would change their minds."

Rachel's eyes widened.

"But they took everything," Rivka said softly. "The books. The songs. Miriam."

The kitchen clock ticked on. The bread rose silently in the warm oven.

"After the war," Rivka continued, "someone who remembered—someone who cared—found this piano in a shop across the sea. They sent word to me. I did not save it because it was valuable. I saved it because it remembered."

Rachel placed her small hand beside her mother's on the wood. Together, they touched the memory.

"And now," Rivka said, her voice fierce and impossibly gentle, "it sings again. Through you."

Later that evening, the apartment was full—aunts and uncles squeezed around the Seder table, cousins dangling off chairs too big for them, the candles glowing against windows steamed from the cooking.

Rachel perched at the upright piano, knees knocking together under her dress, clutching her sheet music with damp fingers.

Rivka caught her daughter's eye and gave a small nod. Steady as a candle flame.

Rachel lifted her hands. She began.

The first few notes wobbled. The next ran too fast. Halfway through *Eliyahu Hanavi,* she lost her place and had to start the phrase again.

A ripple of chuckles moved through the room — not unkind, but familiar, affectionate. Rachel's cheeks burned. She pressed her lips together.

And kept playing.

The melody found its footing. Her small fingers remembered —

not perfectly, but *truly*.

By the time she reached the end, the room was clapping, a wave of warmth and pride washing over her.

Rachel grinned, jumped down from the bench, and ran straight into Rivka's waiting arms.

"You see?" Rivka whispered into her hair, pulling her close. "It is not about playing perfect."

Rachel looked up, still glowing. "It's about remembering?"

Rivka kissed her forehead. "It's about being free."

Behind them, the family lifted their wine glasses toward the open door, singing into the night:

Eliyahu Hanavi, Eliyahu Hatishbi...

Elijah the Prophet, Elijah the Tishbite...

Rachel squeezed her mother's hand, the music rising around them — imperfect, strong, completely alive.

The piano stood gleaming under the lamplight, waiting for all the songs yet to come.

Much later, when the apartment had gone quiet again—after the last matzo crumbs were swept from the table, after the last aunt kissed Rachel's sleeping forehead—Rivka returned to the piano.

The challah was wrapped under linen on the counter. The Passover candles burned low in their glass cups.

Rivka sat, not bothering with sheet music, her fingers moving with the easy intimacy of memory. She played *Eliyahu Hanavi* again — not for show, not for applause.

For Miriam.

For Rachel.

For herself.

The old upright trembled slightly under her hands, not from weakness, but from the burden it carried so willingly: a village that no longer stood, a song that refused to be lost, a freedom woven not from grand victories, but from small, stubborn acts of remembering.

Outside the window, the spring night stretched quiet and deep.

Inside, Rivka played on, each note a braid of sorrow, survival, and hope, weaving past and future into something that could not be broken.

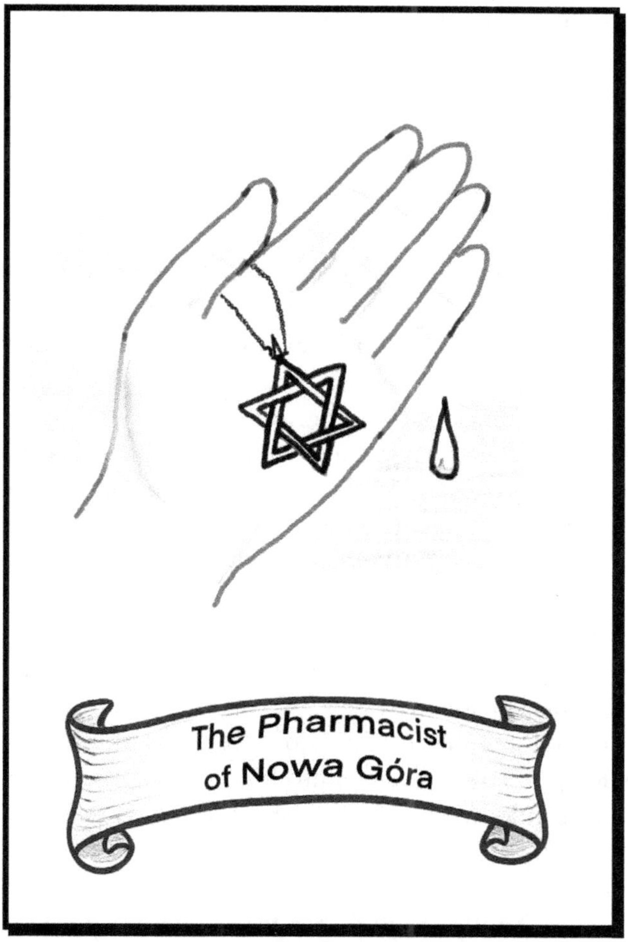

Zofia placed a comforting hand on the boy's shoulder, her fingers gentle but firm as she applied the ointment to his chest. Aron winced, but didn't pull away, his wide eyes fixed on the floor. Across the room, his mother, Sara, hovered anxiously, clutching her shawl tight against her thin frame.

"He's been coughing through the night again," Sara said, her voice cracking. "I don't know what to do, Zosia. I don't know how to help him."

Zofia kept her voice calm, even though her heart ached. The medicines were nearly gone, the herbs dwindling to almost nothing.

But she couldn't let Sara see her worry. "He'll be all right, Sara. You're doing everything you can. Keep him warm, and give him this twice a day."

Sara nodded, taking the medicine and tucking it under her shawl. "Thank you, Zosia. I will."

"You're very welcome. I must go to the bakery. I'll see you tomorrow."

The village of Nowa Góra had grown quieter with each passing day. The once-bustling market square, where children had run between stalls and mothers had bartered for bread, now stood in uneasy silence. Zofia walked slowly, and her mind drifted. Fear had settled over the village like a fog—thick, suffocating, and impossible to escape.

In the square, the air was heavy with whispers. Zofia knew that people still came to her for remedies, but they spoke in hushed voices, glancing over their shoulders as though the shadows themselves were listening. They all knew the same thing: the soldiers would come. They always did.

Zofia heard a light patter behind her as Sara caught up.

"Zosia, I don't know what to do. Aron... he's so sick, and now they say the soldiers are coming."

Zofia placed a reassuring hand on her arm. "You're doing all you can, Sara. Keep him warm, keep him close. We'll figure this out."

Sara's eyes filled with tears, but she nodded. "I don't want him to see what's coming."

"He won't, Sara. I promise you."

Sara smiled faintly through her tears. She grasped Zofia's hand briefly and turned back toward the pharmacy.

At the edge of the square, Zofia saw Moshe Kagan working quietly, fixing a cart with his worn hands. His face was weathered, showing the strain the past three years. Zofia knew he was hiding some of the village boys in his workshop.

Moshe greeted her with a small nod. "Zosia." His voice was low, eyes darting around to make sure no one was listening.

"Moshe," she replied, her smile tight. She knew better than to ask him anything openly, but the lines of worry etched into his face told her everything she needed to know.

Leaning against a crumbling wall near the synagogue,

seventeen-year-old David Lewinsky raised his head. His eyes followed his cousin Zofia as she approached. Zofia started to smile, but her smile froze on her face as David spoke.

"Zosia, I'm going to leave," he said suddenly, his voice tight with fear and resolve. "I can't stay here. They'll come for us all."

Zofia looked at him sharply. "Where will you go, David?"

He shrugged. "Anywhere. Somewhere safer. There has to be a way."

Zofia softened, placing a hand on his shoulder. "There's nowhere safer than here. Stay close to your family."

David clenched his jaw, but he nodded, defeated.

As Zofia walked away, she heard a familiar laugh. Walking a few more steps, she saw her little sister Rivka playing with another child near the square. Even at four, Rivka knew to stay out of sight of the soldiers. But she was laughing.

Rivka ran over to her sister, her face beaming. "Zosia! Look what I found!" She held up a small white flower. "I picked it from the field. Isn't it pretty?"

Zofia knelt down to take it, smiling despite herself. "It's beautiful, Rivkeleh."

Rivka tucked the flower into Zofia's hair and ran back to play.

Zofia approached the small bakery, where Yosef Stein stood outside, wiping flour from his hands. He looked up, offering a small but weary smile.

"Good afternoon, Zosia," Yosef greeted her, though his voice carried little of its usual warmth. "I've got some bread for you."

"I appreciate it, Yosef." She handed him a few coins, though she knew he'd never ask for payment.

Yosef lowered his voice as he wrapped the bread. "The soldiers came by again. Asking questions."

Zofia's stomach tightened. "Did they say anything new?"

He shook his head. "No. But it's only a matter of time before they start asking harder questions."

She nodded, taking the bread. "Stay safe, Yosef. We'll need you."

The warm scent of bread filled the air, but today it did nothing to comfort Zofia. The soft clinking of coins, the murmur of voices—everything in Yosef's bakery felt muted. Zofia stood at the counter, waiting for her loaf, when the door creaked open.

The room fell silent.

Heinrich Vogel walked in, his boots echoing loudly on the stone floor. Yosef froze, his hands gripping the bread knife a little too tightly. The other customers shifted nervously, eyes darting to the floor, avoiding Vogel's gaze. Helena pulled her shawl tighter around her shoulders. Staszek shifted from foot to foot, his large hands clasped together. Young Ania, barely out of her teens, stood quietly by the counter, staring wide-eyed at the officer and clutching her basket.

Zofia straightened, her heart quickening. She kept her expression calm, though every muscle in her body wanted to run.

He can't know. He's just here for bread. Don't give him anything.

Vogel's gaze swept over the small crowd before settling on Zofia. A slow, deliberate smile spread across his face as he approached her.

"Guten Tag, Fräulein Lewinski."

His tone was polite, almost friendly, but the weight of his presence was undeniable. He stepped closer, inspecting the loaves on display with exaggerated care.

"Guten Tag, Herr Offizier," Zofia said, careful to keep her voice measured.

Behind the counter, Yosef's hands shook as he sliced another loaf, his knuckles white against the handle of the knife. Zofia could feel the tension rolling off him, but she couldn't let it show in her own face.

Vogel picked up a loaf, inspecting it as though it were a rare delicacy. His smile remained fixed, his eyes cold.

"Your pharmacy is well regarded in this town. People trust you." He placed the bread back on the counter, his gaze never leaving hers.

"I help the sick when I can."

Her voice was even, but her mind raced. *What does he want from me? Why is he here?*

The customers remained still, as though even the slightest movement would draw his attention to them.

Suddenly, Vogel's tone changed. He leaned in, his smile fading slightly as he switched to Polish.

„Powiedz mi, ilu mężczyzn jeszcze zostało w wiosce?" *Tell me, how many of the men are still in the village?*

Yosef paused, his hand stilling over the bread. The soft clatter of a knife hitting the counter broke the silence. Staszek stiffened beside

Zofia, his jaw clenched, and Ania flinched as though the officer's words had struck her.

Zofia kept her breathing steady. *He's testing me. He wants me to slip.*

"I wouldn't know. People come and go," she said, meeting his gaze, refusing to look away, though her stomach twisted in knots. She could feel Yosef watching her, his fear palpable.

Vogel tilted his head slightly, his smile returning, but his eyes were sharper now.

"Surely the pharmacist knows everyone."

Zofia felt her pulse quicken, but she held her ground. Don't break. Don't let him see your fear. She glanced at Helena, who clutched her basket of bread like a shield. The woman's lips were pressed into a thin line, her eyes pleading. Zofia knew what was at stake—not just for her, but for them all.

"The town is full of good people, Herr Offizier," she said, switching back to German, keeping her voice steady.

Vogel chuckled softly, his gaze drifting lazily over the room. He seemed to take pleasure in the fear he spread like a poison in the air. Ania stood frozen, her eyes wide and filled with uncertainty.

"Good people can be very helpful. And you will be helpful, won't you, Fräulein Lewinski?"

The question lingered, heavy with expectation.

Yosef's knife slipped, and he cursed softly under his breath, though the sound seemed to echo in the suddenly too-small room.

"If I can help, I will." She felt the words burn in her throat. *What else can I say?* Her palms were slick with sweat, her fingers gripping the edge of the counter for stability.

Vogel leaned in, his voice dropping to a near whisper. "I'll return, Fräulein. We will speak more openly next time."

His tone was light, but the warning was clear. With a final glance around the bakery, he turned on his heel and left, the heavy door creaking shut behind him.

The silence in the bakery was suffocating. Yosef let out a shaky breath and leaned heavily against the counter. One by one, the customers stirred, faces pale, hands unsteady.

"Be careful, Zosia," Yosef said, his voice hoarse. "He doesn't just want our names. And…that man doesn't forget."

Zofia nodded. She knew what had happened in other villages. *Forced labour. Arbeitslager.* Disappearances. People erased.

Helena stepped forward, her face pinched with worry. "Thank you, Zofia. You're so brave." Her voice trembled, as though the words were too heavy to carry.

Staszek nodded in silent agreement. "You did the right thing."

Zofia forced a smile, though inside, her heart was pounding. *They're all looking to me. But what if I fail them?*

She picked up her bread, her hands shaking. The others began to leave, Ania casting a last, fearful glance at the door before slipping out into the street. Helena followed, pulling her shawl tighter as though it could protect her from what was to come. Staszek walked out last, his broad shoulders hunched, as if the weight of his survival was too much to bear.

They're counting on me. All of them. If I break...

She closed her eyes for a moment, willing herself to breathe.

He'll be back. And next time, he'll want more. But I won't let him win. I can't.

The synagogue was quiet, its air heavy with the weight of history. The soft glow of late afternoon light filtered through the small, dusty windows, casting long shadows across the stone floor. Rabbi Jakub stood near the bimah, his hands resting lightly on the ancient scrolls before him. His eyes were kind but tired, his face lined with worry that deepened when he saw Zofia approaching.

Zofia stepped inside, the door creaking softly as it closed behind her. She had come seeking guidance, though part of her already knew what must be done.

"Rabbi, I—" She hesitated, swallowing back the fear that had been gnawing at her since Heinrich Vogel had spoken to her in the bakery. "I don't know what to do. They'll come for me, and they'll want more than I can give."

Rabbi Jakub nodded gravely. "They've already taken more than anyone should have to give."

He stepped away from the scrolls, his hands clasped behind his back as he walked toward her. He motioned for her to sit, but Zofia remained standing, her thoughts too restless to settle.

"I don't want to be a coward," Zofia continued, her voice tight with emotion. "I want to protect them. The men, the boys, the people who come to me for medicine... but if I refuse—" Her voice faltered, and she quickly regained control. "If I refuse, they'll kill me."

"They might," Rabbi Jakub replied quietly. He regarded her for a long moment before speaking again, his tone soft but firm. "Some things are worth more than survival."

Zofia flinched slightly at his words, though they were said with kindness. The weight of their meaning hung between them, heavy and unspoken.

What could be worth more than survival? Her mind immediately went to Rivka, her little sister. *If I die, who will protect her?*

Rabbi Jakub seemed to sense her thoughts, his expression softening as he spoke again. "Zofia, you are not responsible for the evil they bring into this world. But you are responsible for what you do in the face of it."

He moved closer, his voice low but steady. "I cannot tell you what choice to make. I can only tell you that standing firm, even in the face of death, is the greatest act of defiance there is. Your people need you... but you must decide what is worth the risk."

Zofia's breath caught in her throat. The room felt too small, the air too thick. She wanted to argue, to tell him that Rivka needed her more, but the words wouldn't come. Instead, she pressed a hand to her chest, her heart pounding.

"If I die, they will still come," Zofia said, her voice barely above a whisper. "They'll take more. They always take more."

"Yes, they will." Rabbi Jakub nodded, his face grave. "But your refusal to give them what they want... that will echo long after they've taken all they can."

Zofia stood in silence for a moment, her mind drifting to Rivka. Her little sister, who still believed there was good in the world. *What will happen to her if I'm not here?*

"You are not alone, Zofia," Rabbi Jakub said gently. "There are others who can protect Rivka, others who will continue this fight. But they will need you to be strong now, so that they, too, can be strong."

Zofia looked up at him, tears welling in her eyes. She blinked them back, refusing to let them fall. She knew he was right, but it didn't make the fear any less real.

"Do you really believe that sacrifice can change anything?" Zofia asked, her voice trembling. "That it will matter?"

Rabbi Jakub smiled softly, though the sadness in his eyes remained. "I do. Because every act of defiance reminds us that we are not yet broken. And that is something no enemy, no matter how powerful, can ever take from us."

Zofia left the synagogue, her mind heavy with the rabbi's words. The streets of Nowa Góra were quiet, the evening settling in. She walked slowly, her thoughts a whirlwind of fear, anger, and uncertainty.

Some things are worth more than survival.

The words echoed in her mind, but she still wasn't sure what to do. She thought of Vogel's cold smile, his veiled threats, and the danger that loomed over everyone she cared about.

As she neared the edge of the village, her thoughts returned to Rivka. Her little sister's safety had always been her first priority. *If I die, who will protect her?*

Zofia didn't have an answer, but she knew one thing for certain: she couldn't allow herself to break. Not yet.

They need me.

Rivka needs me.

The small house was quiet, save for the soft crackle of the fire in the hearth. Shadows danced across the walls as Zofia sat at the small kitchen table, her hands folded tightly in her lap. Rivka sat across from her, her legs swinging beneath her chair, her small face illuminated by the warm glow of the fire.

For a moment, the scene almost felt normal—just two sisters, together at the end of the day. But the air was thick with the weight of what was coming. Zofia had known for hours now that this could be the last night they would ever have together. The thought was unbearable.

Rivka looked up at her, her wide, innocent eyes searching Zofia's face for answers.

"Zosia," she asked softly, her voice trembling just enough to make Zofia's heart break, "will the soldiers come for you?"

Zofia's breath caught in her throat. She had been dreading this moment, but Rivka was smart. She had seen too much already. There was no point in pretending.

Zofia forced a smile, though it felt hollow. "No, Rivka," she lied gently, "not tonight."

Rivka frowned, her small hands curling around the edge of the table. "Like they took Mama and Papa. Will they take you, too?"

Like they took Mama and Papa. The words hung in the air, heavy and final. Zofia felt a lump rise in her throat, but she swallowed it down. She had to be strong—for Rivka's sake.

How do I protect her from this? How do I prepare her for what might come?

Zofia reached across the table, taking Rivka's hands in hers. They were small and soft, so fragile compared to the hard, calloused hands of the world around them.

"No matter what happens, Rivka," Zofia said softly, her voice trembling, "I want you to be brave. Can you do that for me? Can you be brave, just like you were when..."

Her voice trailed off. The memory of Mama and Papa's arrest was still too fresh, the pain too sharp.

Rivka nodded, her lips trembling. "I can be brave," she whispered, but her eyes filled with tears.

Zofia's heart shattered.

What will happen to her if I'm not here? What will she do?

"Good girl," Zofia whispered, brushing a tear from Rivka's cheek with her thumb. She tried to smile again, but it felt more like a mask, a thin veneer over the terror building inside her.

How do I say goodbye to her? How do I tell her that everything will be all right, when I don't even believe it myself?

The fire crackled again, and the warmth of the room seemed to mock the coldness settling in Zofia's chest. She had tried to protect Rivka for so long, but now... now, there was nothing left to protect her from what was coming.

She stood, walking around the table to where Rivka sat. Zofia knelt beside her, pulling her little sister into her arms. Rivka clung to her, burying her face in Zofia's neck. Zofia closed her eyes, breathing in the scent of her sister's hair—so familiar, so precious.

This could be the last time I hold her.

Tears burned behind her eyelids, but she forced herself to stay calm. For Rivka. Always for Rivka.

"Do you remember," Zofia began, her voice a soft whisper in the stillness of the room, "what Mama used to say when you were scared?"

Rivka sniffed, nodding slightly against Zofia's shoulder. "She used to say... she used to say that no matter what happens, the sun will rise again."

Zofia's heart squeezed painfully. "That's right," she whispered. "The sun will rise again. And no matter what happens, Rivka, you will always be safe in my heart."

But will she be safe in anyone else's? The thought sent a fresh wave of fear through her. She had no idea if anyone in the village could take Rivka in, could hide her. Vogel's presence loomed large in her mind, a dark shadow that threatened to steal everything.

Rivka shifted in her arms, pulling back slightly to look up at her. Her big eyes, so full of trust, gazed into Zofia's.

"Zosia... are you scared?"

Zofia swallowed hard, the truth lodged like a stone in her throat. But she couldn't lie. Not now. Not about this.

"Yes," she whispered. "I'm scared. But we can't let fear stop us from being strong."

Rivka nodded, but the tears were back, slipping down her cheeks despite her best efforts to be brave.

Zofia kissed the top of her sister's head, cradling her tightly. *What if this is the last time?* The thought pounded in her mind, but she pushed it aside.

For tonight, they were still together. For tonight, Zofia could still protect her.

Zofia stood by the doorway, watching as Rivka slept, her small form curled beneath the blankets. The house was so quiet, so still. The fire in the hearth had died down to embers, and the cold was beginning to creep in.

Zofia's heart felt like it was breaking into a million pieces. What if this is the last time I ever see her like this? So peaceful, so innocent?

The rabbi's words echoed in her mind. *Some things are worth more than survival.*

But here, standing in the doorway, looking at her sleeping sister, nothing seemed worth more than this—than protecting Rivka.

She clenched her fists at her sides, her nails digging into her palms.

I will not let them take her. No matter what happens to me, Rivka will survive. She has to.

The air in the small pharmacy felt thicker than usual. Zofia stood behind the counter, her heart pounding, but she kept her posture steady. She had known this moment was coming ever since Heinrich Vogel had left his ultimatum hanging in the air the day before.

The door creaked open, and Vogel stepped inside, his polished boots echoing against the floor. He paused for a moment, surveying the room before his gaze landed on her. His expression remained polite, but Zofia saw the coldness in his eyes.

"Good evening, Herr Offizier," Zofia said, her voice even.

Vogel's lips twisted into a thin smile as he approached. "Fräulein Lewinski, I believe we have unfinished business."

Zofia nodded, bracing herself. *I know what you're going to ask. And I already know my answer.*

Vogel leaned forward, placing his hands on the counter. "I've been patient with you. You've had time to think. Now, I'm going to ask you one last time. Give me the names of the Jewish men and boys."

His words were delivered as if he were asking for nothing more than a simple favor.

Zofia's fingers tightened on the counter. Her voice was firm. "I cannot give you those names, Herr Offizier."

Vogel's smile disappeared. He straightened, his eyes narrowing. "Cannot? Or will not?"

Zofia met his gaze, her heart racing. "Will not."

Silence hung between them for a long moment before Vogel sighed and shook his head.

"You're making a dangerous choice, "Fräulein Lewinski."

He began to pace, his hands clasped behind his back. "You're choosing them over yourself. Over your sister."

A chill ran down Zofia's spine, but she didn't flinch.

"If protecting them means I must give my life, then so be it," Zofia said quietly.

Vogel stopped pacing and turned to face her. His voice lowered to a near whisper. "You think this is about sacrifice? Martyrs don't save anyone. They only die."

Zofia's hands trembled, but she didn't break. "I will not give you what you want."

Vogel's smile returned, colder than before. "You've sealed your fate. Your defiance will not be tolerated. Tomorrow, you'll pay the price."

The walk to the house was cold and quiet. The moonlight cast long shadows over the cobblestones, and every sound seemed amplified in the stillness. Zofia held Rivka's hand tightly, her heart aching with every step.

When they reached Sara's house, Zofia knocked softly, her pulse racing. Sara opened the door, her face filled with concern.

"Zofia? What's happening?"

Zofia's voice trembled. "I need you to take Rivka tonight. Please, Sara. Just for tonight."

Sara's eyes widened as she looked between the two sisters, understanding the urgency. She nodded quickly and stepped aside to let them in.

"Of course. Come in."

Inside, Sara knelt down in front of Rivka, offering a gentle smile. "You'll be safe here with me tonight. We'll have tea, and maybe you can help me bake in the morning."

Rivka looked at Zofia, her voice trembling. "Will Zosia be all right?"

Zofia forced a smile, though it felt like her heart was breaking. "I'll come for you in the morning, Rivkeleh. I promise."

She turned to Sara, her voice low. "Keep her safe. No matter what happens."

Sara nodded, her expression grave. "I will, Zofia."

Zofia knelt beside her sister, pulling her into a tight embrace. "Be brave for me, okay?"

Rivka nodded, her eyes filled with tears. "I will."

Zofia kissed her forehead and stood, feeling as though her heart was being torn from her chest. As she walked out of Sara's house, Zofia knew she might never see her sister again.

The house felt unbearably quiet now, the absence of Rivka like a heavy weight pressing down on Zofia's chest. The small space, which had once been filled with the sound of her sister's laughter, was now suffocating in its stillness. Zofia stood in the doorway for a moment, staring into the empty room, before closing the door behind her with a soft click.

The day's events, the confrontation with Vogel, and the hurried goodbye to Rivka replayed over and over in her mind, like a scene she couldn't escape. *I did what I had to. But is it enough? Will Rivka be safe?*

Zofia moved slowly through the house, her hand trailing over the back of the chair where Rivka had sat just that morning. Everything felt so ordinary, so painfully familiar, and yet she knew nothing would ever be the same again. The air felt heavier, as if the walls themselves understood what was coming.

They'll come in the morning. There's no doubt now. Vogel won't give me another chance.

She inhaled deeply, trying to steady herself. *I've done all I can for Rivka. Now, I just have to be strong enough to face what's next.*

Zofia walked over to the small table by the window, lighting a single candle. The soft glow flickered against the walls, casting shadows that danced with the breeze coming through the cracks in the windowpane. She sat down, her hands trembling slightly as she rested them on the table. Her mind was racing, each thought more frantic than the last.

What will they do to me? How long will it take for them to find out I won't break?

She glanced at the door, half-expecting the soldiers to come bursting through it already. But the night was still. The silence of the village outside only added to the tension building inside her chest.

Zofia reached into the drawer beside her, pulling out a small stack of papers—medical records, documents, lists of people she had helped. She stared at them for a moment, her thumb brushing over the edges. *They won't take these. Not if I can help it.*

She walked toward the wood stove, her footsteps quiet but firm. Opening the stove door, she paused for a brief second, feeling the weight of the life she had built in those papers. With a deep breath, she struck a match and set it to the corner of the stack. The flame caught quickly, flickering and growing as it devoured the pages.

As she watched her life's work go up in flames, Zofia felt a strange sense of finality and, oddly, relief. She closed the stove door, the fire's glow casting long shadows behind her.

Her thoughts drifted back to Rivka, now safe at Sara's house, and her heart squeezed with a mix of relief and sorrow. *At least she'll be safe. At least I've done that.* But what would happen to Rivka once the soldiers took her away? Would Sara be able to keep her hidden? Would the village protect her?

The questions hung in the air, unanswered and heavy.

Zofia stood and moved toward the window, gazing out into the night. The moon hung high in the sky, casting a pale light over the cobblestone streets. The village was still, but Zofia could feel the tension building beneath the surface. Heinrich Vogel had promised to return, and when he did, she knew there would be no more time. No more waiting.

She pressed her palm against the cool glass, closing her eyes for a moment as the weight of it all pressed down on her. *I've done everything I could. Now, I just have to face what's coming.*

Zofia turned back to the room, her gaze falling on the small bed she shared with Rivka. The blanket was neatly folded at the foot, just as it always was, but the sight of it sent a fresh wave of grief through her. She walked over to it slowly, sitting down on the edge and resting her hands in her lap. Beneath the mattress, she kept a small box—her mother's pendant, the Star of David. The only thing left from the life they had before the war.

Zofia pulled the box out and opened it, the metal of the pendant cool against her fingers. She held it for a long moment, the memories of her mother flooding back. The warmth of her embrace, the sound of her laughter. The life they had lost.

With trembling hands, Zofia slipped the necklace over her head, letting it rest against her chest. *For Rivka. For Mama.* She closed her eyes, feeling the weight of it. *I can't be afraid now. There's no time for fear.*

She stood and moved back to the window, staring out at the village once more. She could almost feel the eyes of the villagers on her, even though the streets were empty. They were counting on her, whether they knew it or not. They were counting on her to keep her promise, to protect them even when it meant losing everything.

Some things are worth more than survival. The rabbi's words echoed in her mind, and she felt a strange sense of peace settle over her. *I won't give them the names. No matter what happens to me, I won't betray them.*

Zofia inhaled deeply, holding her breath for a moment before releasing it slowly. The morning would come soon enough. When it did, she would be ready.

The sun had barely risen when the knock came at the door. Zofia had been awake all night, sitting by the window, watching the darkness give way to the dull light of dawn. She knew who it would be. Heinrich Vogel had made it clear. There would be no escape, no second chances.

The knock was sharp, impatient, and it echoed through the small house. Zofia stood, her heart steady now, though her legs felt weak beneath her.

This is it. This is the moment.

Her mind flashed to Rivka, tucked safely away at Sara's house. *At least she'll be safe. At least I've done that.*

Zofia opened the door slowly. As expected, Vogel stood on the threshold, two soldiers flanking him. His expression was unreadable, but there was a hardness in his eyes that told Zofia there would be no more games.

"Guten Morgen, Fräulein Lewinski," he said, his voice calm. "You've made your choice."

Zofia said nothing, simply nodded. She stepped back from the door, allowing the soldiers to enter. Her heart raced, but she kept her composure. There was no point in fighting now.

Vogel stepped inside, his eyes scanning the small room. He gave a brief, cold smile. "Very well. You'll come with us."

Zofia took one last look around the room—the home she had shared with Rivka, the small space that had been her world for so long. *This is the end of it.*

One of the soldiers stepped forward, grabbing her arm roughly. Zofia winced but didn't resist. Vogel watched with cold detachment as the soldiers moved to escort her outside. The door creaked as it opened, the sunlight flooding the room in harsh contrast to the darkness of the moment.

As they pulled her outside, Zofia caught a glimpse of Yosef across the street, standing by the bakery. His eyes were wide with horror, but he did not move. No one moved. The village had fallen silent, the weight of what was happening pressing down on every soul.

I did what I had to. I didn't give them the names. I didn't betray them.

The town square of Nowa Góra was filled with people. The familiar faces of her neighbours and friends had been drawn into the square, watching in silence as the soldiers prepared the wooden platform. The gallows stood tall and ominous against the gray sky, a stark reminder of the price of resistance.

Zofia stood in the middle of it all, her hands bound, but her head held high. She felt the cold wind brush against her skin, the roughness of the rope cutting into her wrists. Vogel was standing off to the side, watching with his arms folded. His expression was as cold and unreadable as ever, but Zofia sensed his satisfaction. *He got what he wanted. Not the names, but this—a spectacle.*

The soldiers moved with precision, their faces blank as they secured the rope around her neck. Zofia didn't flinch. Her eyes remained fixed on the crowd—the people she had spent her life protecting.

This is it. This is how it ends.

She scanned the faces in the crowd. Yosef, the baker, stood at the front, his eyes wide and filled with horror. Sara, the woman who had taken in Rivka, clutched her shawl tightly, her knuckles white. They all looked at her with a mixture of fear and sadness, but no one moved. No one spoke.

I'm doing this for you. All of you.

Zofia inhaled deeply, her mind racing. Rivka's face flashed in her thoughts, the little girl who still believed in the goodness of the world. *I hope she's safe. I hope she never has to see this.*

The thought tightened the knot in her stomach, but she quickly pushed it away. *This is for her too. This is so she'll have a future, even if I won't.*

Vogel stepped forward, his cold gaze locking with hers. His voice was calm, detached.

"Is there anything you'd like to say, Fräulein Lewinski?"

Zofia met his gaze, her heart pounding in her chest. She knew this was the moment—the moment he had been waiting for. He wanted her to beg, to plead for her life. But she wouldn't give him that satisfaction.

"No." Her voice was steady, even though her body trembled. "I have nothing to say to you."

Vogel tilted his head slightly, his expression unreadable. "Very well."

As Vogel stepped back, Zofia's gaze drifted to the crowd once more. She saw the children—the boys she had refused to betray—standing near the back, their wide eyes filled with confusion and fear. *They don't understand yet. But one day, they will.*

The platform beneath her feet felt unsteady, but Zofia kept her head high. *Some things are worth more than survival.* The rabbi's words echoed in her mind, giving her the strength she needed to face what was coming.

What will they remember of me? She wondered if, years from now, anyone would speak her name. Would they tell stories of the pharmacist who had refused to give the Nazis what they wanted? Or would she be forgotten, just another casualty in a war too big for any one person to stop?

Her thoughts drifted back to Rivka, her sweet little sister. *I did this for you.* A single tear slipped down Zofia's cheek, but she didn't wipe it away. *I hope you understand one day.*

The crowd watched in silence. Some were crying, while others stood frozen in disbelief. Yosef looked like he was about to collapse, his hands shaking. Sara had turned her face away, unable to watch. But Zofia could still feel their presence, their silent support. *I did this for you.*

Vogel stepped forward again, his voice carrying over the silent square. "Let this be a lesson to all who think they can defy us. This is what happens when you resist."

The rope tightened around Zofia's neck, but her thoughts remained clear. She closed her eyes, inhaling one last breath of the cold, crisp air. Then her voice rose, musical, in a song that transcended terror, transcended death:

Shema Yisrael Adonai Eloheinu Adonai Echad.

Baruch Shem kevod malchuto l'olam va'ed.

In her final moments, Zofia's thoughts drifted to a memory of her childhood—Mama's arms around her, the scent of fresh bread in the air. Papa's laughter echoing in the small house. Rivka playing beside her, so full of life, so innocent.

I did what I had to do. I didn't give them the names.

The thought, and the memory, brought her peace. She smiled, a soft, bittersweet smile, as the world began to fade around her.

The room was quiet, the only sound the faint ticking of a clock on the wall. Grace sat beside her Bubbe, Rivka, the weight of the story hanging in the air between them. They were in Rivka's modest apartment, filled with the familiar scent of tea brewing in the kitchen. Grace leaned forward, her eyes wide, her heart aching for the woman who had lived with so much loss.

Rivka's hands trembled slightly as she held the delicate teacup in her lap. Her gaze was distant, focused on something far beyond the room, as if she could still see Zofia standing in the square, the gallows looming behind her.

"After they took her," Rivka began softly, her voice barely above a whisper, "I didn't understand. I was just a child, you know? I didn't know what was happening. All I knew was that my sister was gone. And I never got to say goodbye."

Grace listened in silence, her heart pounding in her chest. She had heard fragments of this story before, but never in this much detail. Never like this.

"They took me in," Rivka continued, her voice thick with emotion. "Moshe and his wife. They tried to keep me safe. But the soldiers came for him too. There was no safety left after that."

Grace felt the sting of tears in her eyes, but she didn't let them fall. She reached out, taking her grandmother's hand in hers, squeezing it gently.

"I'm so sorry, Bubbe," she whispered. "I never knew... I never knew it was like this."

Rivka gave her a sad smile, her eyes glistening with unshed tears. "It's not something you talk about, my love. Not even to your own granddaughter." She paused, staring down at her hands. "But you need to know. You need to understand why Zosia did what she did. She wasn't just protecting me. She was protecting all of us. The entire village."

Grace nodded, the weight of the story pressing down on her shoulders. She felt a deep connection to Zofia, even though they had never met. It was as if she could feel the remnants of Zofia's strength coursing through her, passed down through generations.

"I wasn't supposed to be there, you know," Rivka continued softly, her voice barely above a whisper. "I was supposed to be safe, hidden away at Sara's house. But... I sneaked out. I wanted to find her."

Grace's breath caught in her throat. "You were there?"

Rivka nodded, her gaze still distant, lost in the memory. "I hid behind the market stalls, behind the old barrels. I could see everything... but no one could see me. I watched the soldiers take her. I saw them put the rope around her neck."

Her voice trembled as the memory washed over her, raw and unrelenting.

"I didn't understand what was happening," Rivka continued, her eyes welling with tears. "I thought... I thought she would be okay. I thought someone would stop it. But no one did. No one could."

Grace felt her heart break as she listened, her hand tightening around her grandmother's. She couldn't imagine what it must have been like—for a little girl to witness such horror, to see her own sister standing on that platform, powerless to stop what was coming.

"I wanted to scream," Rivka whispered, her voice trembling. "I wanted to run to her, to hold her hand... but I couldn't. I was too afraid. And then... it was over. Just like that."

Her tears fell freely now, and she wiped them away with a shaking hand. "I don't remember how I got back to Sara's house. I think I was in shock. But I knew... I knew she was gone."

Grace felt her own tears welling up, but she stayed quiet, letting her grandmother continue. The image of little Rivka, hiding behind the market stalls, watching her sister's final moments, was almost too much to bear. The pain of that memory was etched deeply into Rivka's soul, and Grace could feel it as though it was her own.

"I never told anyone," Rivka said softly, her voice thick with emotion. "Not even Sara. I was so ashamed... so afraid. I thought... maybe if I had done something, maybe if I had screamed, it would have been different."

Grace shook her head, her voice barely a whisper. "No, Bubbe. It wasn't your fault."

Rivka nodded slowly, though the guilt still lingered in her eyes. "I know. But sometimes... sometimes I can still see her standing there. I can still hear the soldiers... and I can still hear the silence from the crowd."

Grace pulled her grandmother into a tight embrace, holding her as the tears continued to fall. "You were just a little girl," Grace whispered. "There was nothing you could have done."

Rivka held onto her granddaughter, the weight of her grief and guilt finally spilling over after all those years. Grace could feel the depth of her pain, but she also felt something else—something that connected them both to Zofia. It was as if Zofia's spirit still lingered, watching over them, offering her strength from beyond.

After a long silence, Rivka pulled back, her tear-streaked face filled with sorrow and relief. "I never wanted you to know this pain, Grace. But... maybe it's time. Maybe it's time for you to understand."

Grace nodded, her heart heavy with the weight of the story. "I do, Bubbe. And I'm so glad you told me."

Rivka smiled weakly, her eyes still glistening with tears. "She was strong, Grace. Just like you."

Grace took a deep breath, feeling the connection between the past and the present growing stronger. "I hope I can live up to her legacy," she said softly.

Rivka reached out, cupping Grace's cheek. "You already are, my love."

Acknowledgements

The stories in *Threads of Light* would not exist without the foundation laid by *The Second Coming of Grace.* My deepest thanks once again to those who made both journeys possible:

- To my family—thank you for your patience and belief in me, especially on the days when I had none. Your support has carried me farther than you know.

- To my late father, Charles James Eccles—on my sixth birthday, you gave me a dictionary inscribed, "To my daughter...I give the English language." I've been trying to live up to that gift ever since. These stories are one small answer to it.

- To my mother, Dawn Eccles—your strength and resilience have been a lifelong inspiration. Thank you for showing me what endurance looks like in both spirit and body.

- To my sisters, Barbara and Jennifer Eccles and their families—thank you for your unwavering support, both moral and practical, throughout the writing of these stories. I couldn't have done this without you.

- To my great-aunt Finkele, the real pharmacist—your courage, resilience, and story were the spark that inspired *The Pharmacist of Nowa Góra*. It carries your legacy, and I carry you.

- To Bonnie Gillespie and my fellow writers in her group—thank you for your wisdom, encouragement, and the safe space you created for vulnerability and growth. I wouldn't have made it to the finish line without your thoughtful eyes and generous hearts.

- To my teachers, mentors, and writing guides—from the University of Toronto to UCLA Extension, and from actor's stages to the quiet corners of bookstore cafés—thank you for shaping the voice I now write with.

- To the readers and friends who've walked alongside me—those who read early drafts, asked hard questions, or simply listened while I worked through the puzzle—thank you for holding the space.

- And finally, to every person who has ever felt too much, too different, or too alone—these stories were written for you. May you feel seen in these pages.

It has been a joy to continue walking alongside these characters, and I am grateful for everyone who joined me in stepping back into the light.

About the Author

Naomi Vondell is a Canadian author and screenwriter with deep roots in a richly diverse family. Her heritage reflects Jewish, British, Mennonite, and French-Canadian influences, all of which shape her unique perspective on storytelling. Originally from Thunder Bay, Ontario, Naomi has spent most of her adult life in Toronto and is planning to relocate to Victoria, BC, in the near future.

Her debut novel, The Second Coming of Grace, is a spiritual coming-of-age tale about a Toronto actress discovering her clairsentient abilities. It is available on Amazon in paperback and eBook formats. *Threads of Light* continues the journey begun in *The Second Coming of Grace*, delving deeper into the lives and echoes that shaped Grace's world.

When she's not writing, Naomi enjoys sushi, lattes, and cobblestone streets, and looks forward to sharing her home with a couple of cats.

You can contact Naomi at info@naomivondell.com or check out her website, www.naomivondell.com.